LYING

THREE

LYING THREE

by

Ralph McInerny

Thorndike Press • *Thorndike, Maine*

Library of Congress Cataloging in Publication Data:

McInerny, Ralph M.
  Lying three.

  1. Large type books.   I. Title.
[PS3563.A31166L9 1981]   813'.54   81-9001
ISBN 0-89621-304-8   AACR2

Large Print edition available through arrangement with The Vanguard Press.

Cover design by Marc Rosenthal.

For Nan and Bob Shane
Shalom!

1

There were two things Roger Dowling and Phil Keegan did not see in Cub Park that afternoon: the game of the half century and the shot taken at the Israeli consul.

The first came as no surprise. Perhaps the Cub fan secretly wants the north-side team to continue providing lessons in the anguish of loyalty. The second, the shooting, went unnoticed at the time by everyone except those occupying the consul's box. The bullet missed and the consul was spirited out of the park during a botched double play that brought the stadium to its feet in hopeful expectation and kept them there affectionately booing the home team. It was not until evening, three and a half hours after the shooting, that the fact there had nearly been a real tragedy as well as the usual athletic one became known to Father Dowling.

At the time the shooting occurred, Dowling was enjoying a Frostie Malt while his friend, the Fox River chief of detectives, sipped the third of the four beers that were his quota for a game. Beyond the right-field wall, in the open windows of the buildings overlooking the park, residents and their guests, two or three to a window, enjoyed the game without benefit of tickets, while from time to time a trolley passed on an elevated track giving passengers a free and fleeting view of the home field of a club that had not won a pennant since...But only a Cub fan knows how long and he is loath to mention it. The outfield walls were covered with ivy, genuine grass shimmered in the June sunlight, Andy Frain ushers and hawkers of beer and peanuts and ice cream, as well as of the eponymous gum, were busy among the fans. Wrigley Field, as old hands continued to call it, had seldom been the scene of victories for the home team, but it was, Father Dowling thought, one of the most attractive of major-league parks. Winning is not everything. And the Frostie

Malt was delicious.

Unbeknownst to Roger Dowling and Phil Keegan and thousands of other spectators, the lovely ball park had come close to acquiring a far more dubious distinction that afternoon. Apparently it had been the scene of an attempted political assassination.

That, at least, was the description of the event insisted on by Aaron Leib who, together with two security men, had been in the box with the Israeli consul, as Dowling and Keegan learned while watching the evening news.

They had come back to St. Hilary's rectory where Mrs. Murkin had prepared more of a meal than either man had appetite for after nine innings of snacks, but they did it justice and afterward adjourned to the study. Keegan still grumbled about the defeat.

"It was an interesting enough game, Phil."

"I can't enjoy good baseball when it's being played by a team walloping the Cubs."

"Well, the Sox won anyway."

"The Sox!" Phil Keegan's expression suggested that the Chicago White Sox had done nothing to redeem themselves since the 1919 World Series.

Keegan turned on the television while Father Dowling performed a pipesmoker's rite over a briar he was breaking in. Both men were startled to hear of the shot that had been taken at the Israeli consul at the game they had watched. The event, it appeared, would not have become known if it had not been for Aaron Leib. His image appeared on the screen, a handsome man whose dark eyes sparked with indignation.

"This is not the sort of thing that should be hushed up," Leib said. "The consul wanted to keep it quiet but I respectfully disagree. The American public has a right to know when terrorist fanatics begin to turn the playing fields of the United States into battlefields in their insane war against the State of Israel."

"He's a Fox River man," Keegan said.

"I didn't notice a thing," Father Dowling said. But what might not go on in a ball park and be undetected by thousands of potential witnesses? Leib was describing how the security men had gotten the consul and himself out of the box and out of the park.

"Crawling on our hands and knees! I

don't quarrel with the need for that, in the circumstances. But what should infuriate every American is that these were the circumstances in a baseball park in Chicago."

The news passed on to other subjects, but Father Dowling and Phil Keegan were silent, sharing Leib's anger.

"I didn't even know Israel had a consul in Chicago," Roger Dowling said.

"You thought maybe Skokie?" But Keegan was far from being amused. "Leib is a passionate backer of Israel. Fund raiser, that sort of thing."

"I suppose his inference is sound."

"What inference?"

"That the gunman was a terrorist."

"Probably some goddam Arab."

Toward the end of the newscast, the announcer was handed a slip of paper. He read it solemnly. The studio had received a phone call claiming credit for the killing of the Israeli consul from a man identifying himself as a member of Anne and Archy. He seemed puzzled by what he read.

"Haven't heard from that bunch for over a year," Keegan muttered.

"No."

"They're worse than Arabs."

The newsman promised his audience that they would be kept apprised of developments in this startling episode with its possible international ramifications. The remark had the effect both of escalating the importance of what had happened and trivializing it, as if the shooting were some move in a global game, remote and impersonal, having little to do with a particular individual who had been in a particular gunman's sights. Neither Aaron Leib nor the announcer had given the name of the consul.

"They must have thought they got him."

"No doubt that is why he wanted it kept quiet."

"Oh, Leib is right, Roger. You can't keep a thing like that quiet. At any rate, I doubt that anyone could keep Aaron Leib quiet when his dander is up."

Anne and Archy. Strained humorous play on the word anarchy. If the shooting in Cub Park was connected to Fox River by the presence of Aaron Leib in the box of the Israeli consul, the caller who had claimed credit for it had, oddly, brought the matter even closer to St. Hilary's rectory.

2

Part of Billy Herman's charm lay in the fact that he seemed to do everything to prevent Rosemary from taking him seriously, but she had come to think that his facetious façade was a protective device behind which the real Billy was begging to be taken seriously. Her only defense was to treat his banter as banter and pretend she did not see through it. Of course the fact that she had come to know Billy through his sister Sharon, and that she and Sharon had met as they had, put her somewhat at a disadvantage.

"A nose job? Half the girls I know have had them. The other half have big noses." Billy turned his head, looked at her out of the corner of his eye, and gave her his Durante smile. "Yeah, yeah."

"He was Italian," Rosemary said.

"So was Modigliani."

"I'll take your word for it."

"Shall I make reservations at the Hilton? Or at a discreet motel on the Interstate? A bottle of Concord grape, a loaf of unleavened bread, and thou."

"I'm a shiksa."

"Single or double blade?"

"I'm also a Catholic."

"Modigliani wasn't."

"I'll bet he wasn't blonde either."

Billy, seated on her desk, leaned over to examine the part in her hair. "I like blondes no matter what color their hair is."

She sat at her desk in the offices of Fox River Realty, a half-typed letter in her machine, the sound of the Cubs' game filtering from the office of Gladys Lubins. It seemed strange that a game was being played after what had happened at the ball park yesterday. Gladys was the only other person there, but thank God for Gladys anyway. Rosemary's title was Office Manager, which meant that she answered the phone, typed everybody's letters, kept the files, and did everything else but sell. Gladys, thirty-six, had gotten into the real-estate game three years before, had earned seventy-three thousand dollars last year, thus outearning her husband by many tens of thousands of dollars, thus undermining her marriage, thus turning herself into a vociferous if belated exponent of Women's Lib. She urged Rosemary to study, take the exam, get out from behind that typewriter, and make a ton of money selling real estate.

"While you're still single," she added significantly.

Another sort of single was exciting Lou Boudreau at the moment and even Billy was distracted. The runner tried for second, was thrown out, there was confusion at third base, and the single evolved into a double play. Billy groaned theatrically but Rosemary knew he cared little for the Cubs.

"Dinner and a show," Billy persisted. "Tomorrow night. *Arsenic and Old Lace* is playing in a barn. Raquel Welch and some other fine-tuned actresses. What do you say?"

"No."

"I already bought the tickets."

"Give them away."

"Who the hell wants to see Raquel Welch in *Arsenic and Old Lace*?"

"Sharon?"

"Of course she would. That's why I bought four tickets. We'll be a foursome."

The presence of Sharon seemed to promise that it would not be regarded as a real date with Billy, just four young people enjoying one another's company. The thought carried with it such a wrenching memory of innocence that Rosemary agreed.

"Now for Pete's sake, let me get back to work. This is a business office."

Billy got off her desk and smiled winningly at her. Chubby body, chubby face, an aureole of reddish curls.

"Blood is thicker than water," he said. Sharon? More likely an allusion to his belief that as Irish she was a member of the lost tribe of Israel. She shooed him from the office. She would be ready at seven. Yes, go.

Rosemary Walsh. Irish. But her nationality, like the color of her hair and the contour of her nose, was borrowed.

She flicked on her typewriter and continued with the letter Billy's arrival had interrupted. Typing was a skill newly learned a year ago and, like her altered appearance and changed name, it was part of a disguise that separated her from the young woman who had come to

Fox River fifteen months before, in flight from a self she could no longer bear.

But the most decisive separation between her old and new selves had been effected in a parlor of St. Hilary's rectory when Father Dowling had put on a stole and heard her confession. Not that she had failed to tell him everything before that moment, but saying it all again, concisely, acknowledging it before God and his priest, placed it in a different dimension. When Father Dowling pronounced the words of absolution, slowly, deliberately, as if he himself were grasping their meaning for the first time, their incredible profound meaning, she felt she had ceased being Mary Rossi for good. For good. Cosmetic surgery and dyeing her hair had been protective, changing her name had been a surface thing, but to have confessed her sins and received absolution for them truly made her a new person. And afterward she had awaited with dread the obligations Father Dowling would put upon her, obligations that would force Rosemary Walsh to take up the burden of what Mary Rossi had done. To her surprise, to her relief, perhaps even slightly to her disappointment, the priest had told her there was no need for her to do more. It was a topic they were to discuss again and again in the months that followed.

Gladys Lubins came out of her office, shaking her head with disgust. There was no longer the sound of the baseball game.

"It took some doing, but they managed to lose. I still think that gunman was a disgruntled fan, aiming at Wrigley. Those damned Cubs remind me of my husband."

Rosemary knew better than to reply. Just about anybody but his ex-wife would consider Dennis Lubins a success. Gladys was a large rangy woman, her hair an attractive tangle, her squinty eyes turned skeptically on the man's world she was effortlessly conquering.

"Where is everybody?"

Rosemary reached for the calendar on which she kept track of the sales force and Gladys made an impatient gesture.

"Forget it. Who cares?" She looked at her watch. "I'm showing the Evans place at five. Say what you will, Rosemary, a realtor's hours are murder."

Houses were usually shown in the evening or on weekends, when the husband could come along. Even Gladys agreed it was time wasted to show a house to an unaccompanied wife.

"The twits have never made a serious decision on their own and the thought of actually selecting the setting in which they will live out their lives of quiet desperation fills them with alarm. You'd think it was the husband who'll spend twenty-four hours a day in the place instead of her."

Gladys had a way of making a day spent in quiet domesticity sound like a fiendishly devised punishment. As opposed to what, Rosemary wondered. As opposed to the fulfilling boredom of sitting around this office, muttering about the Cubs, waiting for potential buyers to be ready to look at a house?

"He's in town," Gladys announced to the street. She stood, feet apart, arms akimbo, looking out at Filber Street, not one of Fox River's most distinguished. Fox River Realty occupied a house redesigned to accommodate its operations, the house located in a part of the city whose future was bleak. "He" was Mr. Lubins. Gladys never used his name if she could help it and Rosemary had to think to recall it. Dennis. She had never met him.

"Have you seen him?"

"Not on your life. He phoned. He is very good on the phone."

"Isn't he in Washington most of the time?"

"Most of the time. Leaving some of the time to come back here and haunt me."

"Has he remarried?"

"Hah! I half expect him to file for alimony."

Gladys lit a cigarette that she left in the corner of her mouth, smoke lifting toward the acoustical tiles above. She regarded Rosemary through half-shut eyes. "Was that Billy Herman I heard out here a while ago?"

Maybe it wasn't fair, but Rosemary saw Gladys as a suburban version of the self she had left behind. Oh, Gladys would never be as tough as Mary Rossi had been in the cruel unisex world that Gladys probably thought was a figment of the journalistic imagination. The supersaleswoman's unrelenting attack on domesticity served to make the thought of a home and family even more attractive than Rosemary already found it. Not that she would ever have those things. Willy nilly, Rosemary was condemned to the sort of life Gladys found liberating. Father Dowling became impatient with her for thinking this way, but she couldn't help it. "You're free," he would tell her. "You ought to marry. Is there anyone?"

"Billy Herman," Gladys repeated. "Walsh and Herman? Forget it, Rosemary. They're supposed to be great family men, but don't you believe it. They're as bad as the rest of them."

Gladys took the cigarette from her mouth and Rosemary steeled herself for another account of the great affair that, as much as her success in selling real estate, had spelled the end of Gladys's marriage. If she had left marriage by one door she had fully expected to re-enter it by another. And fast. Gladys had thought they had an understanding but she had filed for divorce and he had not. That was when Rosemary had become Gladys's unwilling confidante. The time was past when it was not clear whether "he" referred to Gladys's husband or to the man who was not going to get a divorce after all. All but the bitterness was in the past. My Jewish lover.

"He's the brother of a friend of mine," Rosemary said. "Sharon and I ..."

"Sure."

Don't argue. Don't call attention to

yourself. Fade into the background. That was her creed. Rosemary aspired to be thought of only as the dependable all-purpose girl, and that is how they did see her, everyone but Gladys with her nutty notion that Rosemary should get into the selling end. Gladys was proof positive that a woman can make big money selling houses. She was also the only one who noticed Billy Herman. Rosemary thought she could detect a grudging respect for Billy, as if Gladys discerned the businessman beneath the comic swain. Once or twice Billy and Gladys had chatted about real estate and Gladys had clearly been impressed by Billy's knowledgeability. Was it only because he was Jewish that she warned Rosemary, all the time thinking of her own sad experience?

"Don't do anything hasty," Gladys said. "How old are you, Rosemary?"

"Twenty-six."

"God, I'd give anything to be twenty-six again."

It would have been a mystery to Rosemary how Gladys ever sold a house if she acted with clients as she did in the office, but with wives and husbands Gladys was a cooing poet of hearth and home, extolling the kitchens and linen closets, the dens and family rooms of the dream house she just had to show this couple. As soon as she laid eyes on it she had thought of them.

The ringing of the telephone saved Rosemary from a recital of what Gladys would do if once again she was twenty-six. "Twenty-six and single," she emphasized, picking up the phone.

Frowning, Gladys took the phone from her ear, looked at it, then brought it again to her ear.

"Are you some kind of creep?"

She slammed down the phone.

"Geez."

"What was it?"

"Some slobbering pervert."

"What did he say?"

"Just be thankful I picked up the phone and not you."

It was a novelty, trying to get Gladys to talk rather than to shut up.

"It wasn't so much what he said as the way he said it."

Rosemary swung back to her typewriter and banged out what would have been a sentence if the machine had been turned on. Gladys looked at her strangely.

"Good Lord, was it for you, Rosemary?"

"Don't be silly."

"It could have been Billy Herman," Gladys teased. "That's it. He thought it was you, he whispered some nutty endearment, and I hung up on him. Rosemary, I'm sorry."

"Gladys, stop it. I've got work to do, for Pete's sake."

"Okay, okay."

Gladys strutted back to her office. Rosemary typed with the machine turned on. The phone call had unnerved her irrationally. Certain as she was no one could find her, she still feared that someday, out of the blue, her past would reappear. And that is how it could happen. A puzzling phone call, meant to make her apprehensive. God help her if they ever found her.

3

In the days immediately following his presence in the Israeli consul's box when a shot had been taken at the diplomat, Aaron Leib made certain the incident would not be quickly forgotten or dismissed.

He appeared on "Kup's Show," he spoke with reporters, Jack Brickhouse interviewed him, the *Fox River Messenger* gave him ample space for his message. This is what Israel has to put up with, Leib would say. Maybe it was even a good thing such an insane attempt had taken place in Chicago, and at a ball game at that; it gave people a sense of what it is like to be a possible target all day long, no matter what one was doing. Aaron Leib hoped this would wake up people to the need to speak out again and again on behalf of Israel's right to survive. It was a lesson some Americans still needed. Some Jews still needed it. And of course politicians needed it most of all.

"You seem to have someone particular in mind," Irv Kupcinet said.

"I'm not here to campaign against Wilfrid Volkser," Leib said, his eyes twinkling at the camera.

"Do I detect the makings of an announcement?"

"Irv, believe me, if I ever have an announcement to make, you'll be the first to know."

In many ways that was an unfortunate exchange, since Leib's indignation came to be seen as a clever testing of a springboard from which to take a dive into politics.

He could afford it. He had been the Plastic King at the age of thirty, expanding a small Fox River operation first statewide and then into adjoining states. "Everything I touch turns to plastic," Leib once said, thereby earning an undeserved reputation for wit. He was the most literal of men. At thirty-six, he sold his interest for millions and the promise to stay out of plastics for five years. He had enjoyed the resultant leisure, engaging in a pursuit of diversion and pleasure every bit as pell-mell as the drive that had made him wealthy, but he developed as well a sense of obligation to his origins. He took up Israel. He became its champion in the Chicago area. He was a tireless advocate and, more to the point, an indefatigable fund raiser. He was off to Tel Aviv at the drop of a hat, sometimes remaining in Israel for weeks. He was said to offer both political and military advice to hosts whose gratitude made them patient with this fervent Midwesterner for whom the Middle East was one more puzzle, the solution to which could be found by undeflected effort and sufficient amounts of money. His own checkbook became known as the Book of Ruthless, he was famous as the man who never took No for an answer from a potential donor to Israel, nor—and this was whispered; Aaron was a family man—from an attractive woman.

"I think the shot was meant for Aaron," someone joked in the bar of the Fox River Club.

"Maybe we *should* send him to Washington."

"He's determined to make it the shot

heard round the world."

"If he takes up one more collection I swear I'm getting baptized."

This apprehension proved prophetic. Aaron Leib let it be known, through Mervel of the *Tribune*, he was planning a benefit that would outclass anything he had hitherto done, with stars of Broadway and Hollywood, Ribicoff and Javits, even the Israeli consul who had been the target of a terrorist shot. Aaron Leib was determined that Fox River, Illinois, should let its voice be heard as never before, no matter the good-natured groaning in the bars and restaurants of Fox River or on the fairways of its golf courses.

On the evening of the second day after the incident in Cub Park, Aaron Leib and Howard Herman set out at 6:30 to play the back nine. Just the two of them, in a golf cart. On the fifteenth fairway, at the sound of a clank of clubs in the bag behind him, Howard Herman turned, ducking his head as he did so. His thought was that some idiot had hit into them without calling "fore." His reaction may have saved his life. The next shot struck Aaron Leib in the back of the head and he fell forward over the controls of the cart. For half a minute the cart wandered erratically around the fairway. Then Howard Herman conquered his horror at the sight of his partner's wound, reached under Aaron, and turned off the key. His frenzied shouting attracted other golfers and within minutes the news was all over the clubhouse. A few more minutes, and it was known in Fox River itself. Aaron Leib had been gunned down on the fifteenth fairway of the Fox River Country Club.

When Phil Keegan arrived at the clubhouse with Cy Horvath, he found Herman sitting on a bench in the locker room still in shock. Several other members of the club were with him but, as Horvath found when Keegan sent him out to the scene of the crime, dozens of others encircled the golf cart or wandered stunned about the fairway. Someone had taken a thin plastic raincoat from Leib's bag and draped it over his body. Horvath, with the aid of the officers from the patrol cars that had sped to the country club, pushed the crowd back, roped off the area with an almost festive-looking barrier provided by the grounds crew, and dutifully awaited the arrival of the medical examiner. The sun in the western sky cast the shadows of the giant trees across the fairway and even as they waited the shadows reached and enveloped the golf cart and the corpse of Aaron Leib concealed beneath the bright yellow plastic raincoat.

In the locker room, Keegan handed Herman a towel. The man still wore golf shoes, one untied, its flap smeared with blood that also stained his left hand.

"When I turned off the key," he said, staring at his hand, then wiping it vigorously. "That's Leib's blood." He looked around vacantly and Keegan found his expression somewhat theatrical.

"Tell me what happened, Mr. Herman."

"Nothing happened. We were heading for Aaron's ball on the fifteenth and all of a sudden..."

All of a sudden there had been the sound in the bag of clubs in the back of the cart and then Aaron pitched forward. Herman described cowering beside his partner while the cart continued to move.

"I kept thinking, this time they got him."

"They?"

"Didn't you hear what happened in the ball park?"

Others joined in and Keegan did not stop the excited talk. The consensus was that the gunman who had missed in Wrigley Field had not missed on the fifteenth fairway.

When the medical examiner came, Keegan went with him to where the body waited. Horvath had the area under control and had already selected several possible angles from which the shot might have been fired.

"Where is the tee, Cy?"

Horvath pointed to the west. The sun, blood red, shone through the trees, looking like Mars is supposed to look. Its size, its closeness, made the universe seem briefly a cozy place. Keegan glanced at the body, which had been uncovered by Bennett, the medical examiner. The back of Leib's head was a mess, but the forehead, when Bennett turned the head, gently as a barber, was worse. Blood, once bright on the grass, was darkening now, and Leib's white slacks were soaked with it too.

"Where are the golf balls?" Keegan asked.

"I've only found one." Cy took it from his pocket. Aaron Leib's name was stamped possessively on the dimpled cover. "It must have been his second shot. This is about four hundred and twenty-five yards from the tee. Not bad in two." Horvath looked around, an odd expression on his face. "I caddied here as a kid."

"A caddy would have seen something."

"What caddy? Those carts made caddies obsolete. Maybe kids nowadays wouldn't want the work anyway."

"Any sign of Herman's ball?"

Horvath shook his head. "It could be anywhere. In the rough, in the trees."

"The trees would have been behind them."

But Horvath had meant a group of evergreens lining a fairway sand trap. "Maybe Herman had already taken his third shot."

Looking toward the green, Horvath's erstwhile caddy's eye saw a ball in the apron of grass just shy of the putting surface. He started toward it and Keegan joined Bennett.

"It passed right through his head," Bennett said. He was chewing gum and betrayed no disgust at the sight before them.

Keegan put two officers to work looking for the slug. Bennett said the body could be taken away now. He'd be downtown.

"Keep in touch," Keegan said.

Two foursomes were waiting on the fifteenth tee as if they expected to continue their game. Keegan sent word that the fifteenth hole was out of play. Golfers! He recalled the joke about George and shook his head. George had had a stroke while playing golf and when others commiserated with George's partner he nodded. "Hit; drag George. Hit; drag George. It was a lousy way to play golf."

One drove from south to north on the fifteenth but because it was a dogleg one headed east into the green. Leib must have hit a towering second shot that ignored the layout of the fairway and took the straight line across the sand trap and the evergreens lining it. Herman, if he had shot toward the bend of the fairway, a much shorter shot, would have been first to hit again. They would have been heading eastward in the cart to where Leib's ball lay, the stand of huge trees behind them.

The last of the sunset filtered through the trees now and Keegan was reluctant to poke around in the failing light, but it seemed as likely a place as any from which the shot had come. It was one of the spots Horvath had selected. Horvath came up now, carrying another ball, presumably Herman's, though it did not bear his name. If it was his, he had been lying three.

"Have the woods posted too, Cy. I want it gone over carefully in the morning."

"You figure this is where he was?"

"We'll see."

Keegan was always reluctant to voice his theories and speculations, even mentally to himself. It was too easy to limit attention by assumptions one is not fully aware of making. Thus, in the locker room, he had heard without accepting the view that there was a connection between Leib's death and the shot taken at the Israeli consul in Chicago two days before. Perhaps. Perhaps not.

Herman had showered and was draped in a towel, smoking a cigar and holding a highball. He was telling new arrivals what had happened on the golf course.

"You and Aaron Leib?" someone said.

"Thank God we had composed our differences," Herman said. "The round was meant to clinch that. Bury the hatchet."

"Did you two go out on the spur of the moment?" Keegan asked. The others stepped back to give officialdom operating room. Herman seemed less amenable to questioning now.

"How do you mean?"

34

"Had you arranged to golf today? Isn't it necessary to reserve a starting time?"

Herman smiled. "Not on weekdays, Captain."

"You mean, not when you're Aaron Leib," someone said.

"Then no one would have known that you and Leib would be on the golf course?"

Herman thought about that. Suddenly his eyes widened. "So how could someone be lying in ambush out there? I don't know. Aaron and I ran into each other in the bar. No, wait, that's not right. We had arranged to meet in the bar."

"When did you arrange that?"

"This morning. Midmorning. My secretary called him."

"Then it would have been known he'd be here this afternoon?"

"If you're asking, did I make an announcement I was going to have a drink this afternoon with Aaron Leib, the answer is no. I don't know who he might have told."

"What time did you arrange to meet?"

"Five o'clock."

"And that's when you met?"

"A little after five. Aaron was late. The

bartender would know when he came in, if it's important." Herman's tone suggested that Keegan was wasting time on trivialities.

"Maybe it is."

Herman looked unconvinced.

"So you met shortly after five. When did you decide to golf?"

Herman hesitated before donning the expression of one deciding to go along with this, whatever his opinion of it. "After six. Before six-thirty perhaps a quarter after six. Not that we left the bar then. Aaron sent someone to check with the starter. We were told there'd be no problem if we played the back nine."

"Whom did he send?"

"The waiter. No. A busboy."

"That was at six-fifteen?"

"Six-fifteen. Six-thirty. Around then."

"And prior to that time no one would have known Aaron Leib would be on the golf course?"

"No, they wouldn't have."

"What was the purpose of your meeting with Aaron Leib?"

"Do you mind if I dress, Captain? I'm beginning to feel a bit ridiculous standing around in a towel."

"Is there some place we can talk? After you dress."

"More questions?"

"Well, Mr. Herman, who knows better than you what happened out there?"

"You're right, of course. I'll meet you upstairs in the lobby in five minutes."

Keegan had not objected to the kibitzers in the locker room since Herman had not, but it was a more typical inquiry that he conducted when he and Herman settled in the manager's office with the door closed to the curious. Horvath had gone off to talk with Mrs. Leib.

"I hope someone is looking into the terrorist angle, Captain," Herman said, crossing his legs and running a thumb and forefinger along the crease of his trousers.

"What differences with Aaron Leib had you composed?"

"Did I say that?"

"Yes."

Herman smiled sadly. "How much do you know about Aaron Leib?"

"Tell me."

The sketch of the dead man was given with grudging admiration. "Leib had been a huge success at an early age. The Plastic

King. He had sense enough to get out young and turn to other things."

"Are you in plastics too, Mr. Herman?"

"Sometimes I wish I were. A joke. No. Fox River Casing. I hope the name means something to you."

"I've heard of it."

"I sponsor the police pistol team, Captain."

"Of course."

"We manufacture small-arms ammunition, shells, grenades."

"Then you and Mr. Leib would not have been talking business?"

"Not my business, certainly. No, we'd had some differences because of his passion for Israel. Don't get me wrong. I buy the idea of a homeland. I back Zionism one hundred percent. Aaron expected more than a hundred percent. He sometimes failed to see that not everyone is as well off as he is. Was. He couldn't stop pressing. In fact, he got pretty vicious. He didn't seem to realize a man has to make a living." Herman paused and then forced a smile. "But you know the saying. Wherever there are two Jews there are three opinions. We were friends. Today I told him so. That's what I mean about composing differences."

"You made an appointment with him to tell him you were still friends?"

"That's simplification but basically, yes, that's right."

"Tell me, Mr. Herman. Who would have shot Aaron Leib?"

Herman stood and drew on his cigar. "That's plain as can be, Captain. Whoever took the shot at the ball park."

It was a theory difficult to discount after the phone call to the *Fox River Messenger*. Anne and Archy claimed credit for the execution of the warmonger Aaron Leib.

4

When Phil Keegan phoned to say he wouldn't be able to make it for cribbage because of the murder of Aaron Leib, Roger Dowling urged his old friend to drop by the rectory anytime before midnight if he cared to.

"I may do that."

"He was shot on the golf course?"

"I'll tell you all about it when I get there, Roger."

"Do you suppose he was the target at Wrigley Field?"

"I don't suppose anything," Phil Keegan said.

And of course he wouldn't, at least he would try not to, but it was going to be difficult to ignore the fact that Aaron Leib had been seated in the Israeli consul's box at the ball park when a shot was taken. No doubt Phil felt an understandable reluctance to see a Fox River slaying turned into an incident in international politics and thus become, for all practical purposes, incapable of solution by the local police.

It was difficult not to admire Phil Keegan's singleminded pursuit of justice. He had a refreshing conviction that those who committed crimes should be apprehended and punished with a minimum of delay and particularly without roiling the waters with what Keegan considered misguided pity. Well, pity and mercy are only similar, they are not the same thing. By pity Keegan meant the tendency to see the criminal as victim, as something less than a wrongdoer. Mercy presupposed fault on the part of its recipient. If there was a difference between Phil Keegan and himself, Father Dowling often thought, it lay in this: Phil's concern was justice while his own was mercy.

For the priest could not avoid thinking of the figure who had lain waiting for his opportunity in one of the houses overlooking the outfield walls of Cub Park. That same man, or another, had waited on the golf course for Aaron Leib and shot him from ambush. How easy to feel dread and fear of such persons; yet it required little imagination to see them as fearful and cowardly, perhaps inwardly disgusted with themselves for the furtiveness with which they acted. Roger Dowling did not see the assassin as a mythical figure nor had he any inclination to absolve him of blame. But as a priest he knew that not even assassins are out of range of God's infinite capacity to pardon and forgive. And, as a priest, mercy and pardon must be his chief concerns. He had been brought by his weakness to see that he himself was in need of that mercy. He had been humbled by alcohol. What had been regarded as a promising ecclesiastical career had been ruined when he could no longer conceal his dependence on drink, and his days on the archdiocesan marriage court had come to a less than glorious end and his appointment to St. Hilary's, not regarded as a plum, had been taken to mark the final chapter in a sad story. But Roger Dowling had come to be grateful for what had befallen him. At St. Hilary's he had created a serene and satisfying life. His parishioners were all the flock he needed; his life as a priest had moved onto a different and more solid stage. Something like peace returned when the anguish of insoluble marital tangles no longer tempted him to the oblivion of drink. No longer able to see himself as a successful careerist, perhaps destined for yet higher things, he had drawn closer to God. He had his pastoral work, his Dante and Thomas and other favorite authors, and he had the friendship of Phil Keegan.

When Rosemary Walsh came to him with her incredible tale, she had found a receptive ear. As time went on, he had been pleased to see her establish a new life, not unlike the way he himself had after being assigned to Fox River. But now he was uneasy for her. The incident at Cub Park had been the beginning. Uneasiness became anxiety when he heard on the radio the terrorist claim to have shot Aaron Leib. Roger Dowling tried unsuccessfully to reach Rosemary at home. Nor did anyone answer when he called Fox River Realty.

He tried to reassure himself with the thought that Rosemary had not gone directly home from work. She was shopping or whatever. He would wait and call again. He turned to his breviary, trying to concentrate, and, when that proved difficult, put down the book and dialed Rosemary's number. No answer. Back to his breviary then, suppressing the thought that it was absurd to sit here repeating the Psalms of David while... While what? He finished Vespers, closed the book, and pressed his palm flat on its leather cover, feeling the thin pages give way under the pressure, air forced from between them. *Breviarium Romanum*. He continued to read the daily office in Latin, hoping it was not prideful eccentricity. Latin provided a connective thread in his priesthood, enabling him to trace back through the years to the young subdeacon who had taken on the obligation to recite the breviary every day, reading from its seasonal compilations of psalms, passages from the Old and New Testaments, and the Fathers. And the beautiful hymns. He loved it. He derived an aesthetic as well as a spiritual satisfaction from mumbling the familiar words. Latin words. In English they lost something, something not merely aesthetic and sentimental. Roger Dowling had no objections to the new vernacular liturgy. It was right for people to pray in their own language. Latin was known by only a few and had perhaps constituted a linguistic barrier. But, dear God, the caliber of the English now used was itself a barrier. Ah, well. He himself could continue to pray in Latin.

He let these thoughts go. Far less than the breviary did they keep his mind from Rosemary.

Keegan would have snorted at his fear that there was a connection between these shootings and Rosemary Walsh. Not that Keegan knew Rosemary. Before or after her cosmetic surgery. She had asked Father Dowling's advice about that.

"It's okay to do it, isn't it, Father? It isn't a sin?"

"It's not a sin."

"I remember a nun speaking once about tattoos."

Father Dowling could imagine the little nunnish *ferverino*, perhaps the more unctuous for being given to girls who were vastly unlikely to be tempted by the tattooist's needle. An abuse of the body, the temple of the Holy Ghost, marking it up like a wall. The sentiment seemed right, whatever one made of the theology. Once in London

Roger Dowling had seen a man, a street haranguer, tattooed from midriff to the top of his shaven head, not a square inch of him unadorned. Grotesque, a willed freakishness, but sinful? Who could say? The nun might have made a better case of the vanity that lies behind cosmetics.

"Oh, she did," Rosemary said. "The one thing she was quite sure was all right was soap."

"Cleanliness and godliness."

Rosemary smiled. She herself had a just-scrubbed look, perhaps the influence of that nun. "It's not out of vanity, Father."

How odd she had chosen that way into her revelations. She had made them in stages, thus adding an unintended note of suspense, building gradually to her reason for fleeing.

Had he been surprised? Not by what she said so much as by the fact that it was someone seated across the table in a parlor of the parish house who had been mixed up in these legendary things, the stuff of journalistic exposés, one more sign of the times. Indeed, it was so sensational that Roger Dowling had been skeptical. It so easily could have been an elaborate neurotic justification for wanting cosmetic surgery. But Rosemary had no need of such surgery. Of course his estimate and her own of whether her appearance was attractive were two quite different things, but Rosemary was more reluctant than eager to have the surgery done.

"It's not like changing my name. Women are raised in the expectation that they will eventually change their name. Not quite like this, of course, but you know."

That was a constant phrase of hers: you know. It seemed a plea rising out of her inarticulate generation and become a habit even with those like Rosemary, who were perfectly capable of explaining to him what presumably he already knew. You know. But he did not know. He understood what she had been involved in, but he could not grasp the why.

"Why?" She repeated the question but seemed to find it foreign. "You mean the reasons? I've told you the reasons."

But the reasons were slogans, explaining nothing. He wanted to know why she had accepted them as reasons. But he did not pursue it. He knew, better than most, perhaps, that the search for motives and reasons has an ending unlike its beginning. One began seeking clarity and ended in the darkness and privacy of the human soul. He himself had been asked why he began to drink and he had been able to describe the circumstances, the pressures, the heartache, that had been his during the long years on the marriage tribunal, considering hopeless case after hopeless case. But others had felt the same and had not turned to drink, just as others had heard the slogans Rosemary had heard and had not embraced them. The human heart is a mystery; our lapses, obscure as they are, more easily understood than our occasional ability to do the good and noble thing. Sin and grace—one did not inquire into these as if they were riddles to be understood.

So Rosemary, who was not Rosemary, made the appointment with the cosmetic surgeon in Skokie, spared a long wait because of a cancellation, and when she next came to the door of St. Hilary's rectory, Mrs. Murkin did not recognize the woman who as Mary Rossi had been there half a dozen times. Would Roger Dowling have recognized her if he had not been alerted by her phone call? He assured her he would not have. Her disguise was complete. But she was not yet free of her past. It was on that occasion he heard her confession.

The tale of bombings, vandalism, harassment, agitation, all the plots and plans and crazy disruptions, repeated as sins for which Rosemary asked forgiveness, culminated in her whispered claim to have committed murder.

He did not question her interpretation as he had when they had been simple interlocutors, a fifty-year-old man who happened to be a priest, a woman in her twenties who had become terrified of terrorism. She had been, however unwittingly, an accessory. In the crazy logic of the life she had led, she could not escape responsibility for the unscheduled explosion that had destroyed half her group and three innocent people in the next apartment. Listening to her, Roger Dowling remembered reading of this incident in the papers, the photographs of the scene reminiscent of those of wartime London. When he gave Rosemary absolution, tears ran from her altered eyes and down the contours of her newly acquired nose.

"Whatever became of that Rossi girl?" Mrs. Murkin asked one day, and Father

Dowling looked to see if his housekeeper suspected anything. But clearly she did not.

"She went home," he said, and Mrs. Murkin was satisfied.

"Such a frightened little thing."

What would Mrs. Murkin have said if she knew of the terror that frightened little thing had inspired in others, before she had come to terrify herself? Mary Rossi had indeed come home. Roger Dowling had watched her make her way slowly and painfully back to what she had lost: her faith, her conviction as to the ultimate meaning of life. Religious belief had enabled her to accept the grim fact that she could not contact her family. Did she have an obligation to talk to the police or the FBI?

Roger Dowling told her she did not.

He had been reinforced in these thoughts when he chatted with Francis X. O'Boyle, a parole officer who lived in the parish. O'Boyle, bearded, compassionate, slightly mad, had gone on and on about prison conditions while behind him on the walkway between the church and rectory Mrs. O'Boyle was being pulled in opposite directions by her ebullient children. She wore a sweet saintly smile while being thus drawn and quartered, her attention on her husband's words. Roger Dowling assumed that O'Boyle's tales of ordinary criminals could be matched by the experience of terrorists in prison.

It was a fine point, and one he would not have wanted to argue with Phil Keegan, let alone with a theologian. A theologian of the old school, that is. The new ones, well . . . But he felt an odd affinity with those innovators who had seemed to play fast and loose with the whiteness and blackness of the moral life, sin and guilt obscured and qualified beyond recognition, the demands of civil society regarded as alien intrusions from a suspect source. Roger Dowling developed no sweeping theories on the matter. Right and wrong were clear enough; it was the imputation of guilt or innocence that was hard. He was content with the certainty that Rosemary Walsh need not turn herself in to the agency that had been pursuing her for years.

The underground had gone, if possible, farther underground. The wave of terrorism ebbed, then seemed to stop, or it crossed the ocean where it raged as it never had in America. From time to time its denizens emerged with fast-talking lawyers at their sides, there was a quick judicial shuffle, and all seemed forgotten, more or less with impunity. It was difficult to think an implacable state still wished to extract a debt from Mary Rossi become Rosemary Walsh. Rationalization? Perhaps. But, again, it was not a comprehensive theory he had, only the conviction that Rosemary's real danger lay with the companions she had deserted. If she made public acknowledgment of what she had done, who would protect her from those who considered her a traitor? Father Dowling was familiar with the riddling ambiguity of human action. Rosemary seemed relieved when he told her that her real duty was to make a new life without endangering herself or those she loved. Her penance? The prayers he asked her to say were scarcely as demanding as the prospect of permanent separation from her family.

"Don't," he advised, when she spoke of visiting Detroit to observe her family from afar.

"They won't recognize me."

"No. But you will recognize them."

He doubted she would have the courage to keep her distance once she saw again the mother and father and brothers and sisters whose hearts she had broken by her notorious deeds.

Was it madness to see a connection between Rosemary's past and these cowardly shootings? Anne and Archy. That was the connection, Rosemary's old group claiming to be behind the shootings. Did their proximity suggest they had tracked down their prodigal sister? Israel. The Middle East had been a leitmotif of Rosemary's tale, an anti-Zionist thread. Who were the hawks on Vietnam, trying to sustain the martial spirit lest they too be abandoned? "Abandoned" was Roger Dowling's word. Rosemary's old companions were convinced Israel was a major cause of the evils they professed to fight.

"They control the Congress," Rosemary said. "That was our belief."

"Not Wilfrid Volkser."

"Who's he?"

"It doesn't matter."

Why should Rosemary know the name of the congressman whose district included Fox River?

5

At the sound of a car in the Herman driveway, Sharon sprang from bed, wrapped herself in a curtain, and looked down in panic as the back door of the cab opened. It seemed hours before anyone got out and when Sharon saw who it was she all but crumpled to the floor in relief.

"My God, it's Rosemary Walsh."

"Hey, that's pretty nice." From the bed where he lay supine in all his male splendor, Norman regarded her with admiration. "The curtain, I mean."

She stepped free of it and began to clamber into her clothes. "Get up, you dink. That might have been my mother. Or my father!"

"Who is Rosemary?"

"I'll be downstairs. Get dressed. And if you come down don't say anything dumb."

"Me?"

"You. Rosemary's a friend of mine."

"Well, any friend of yours..."

Sharon fled the room, buttoning her blouse as she skidded down the carpeted stairs in barefeet. The front door chimes filled the house with their stupid intervals. Rosemary!

When Sharon opened the door, Rosemary's face might have been the mirror of her own. The girl looked frightened to death.

"You're home."

"Good grief, Rosemary, what's the matter?"

"I'll tell the cab to go."

This was all but yelped and Sharon stopped buttoning her blouse as she watched Rosemary indicate to the cabbie that he could leave. She tried to remember what Rosemary had looked like before her operation but the only sure resemblance was the expression in her eyes. Sharon felt uneasy when Rosemary turned to look at her with those penetrating eyes.

"Is Billy here?"

"No. Where's your car? Why the cab?"

Rosemary looked away. They were in the

living room now, which was reflected in the television screen. "It was gone." Rosemary turned. "Someone must have borrowed it."

"*Borrowed* it?"

"You haven't been listening to the radio?"

"Calling all cars? Did Billy ask you to meet him here?"

"Didn't he tell you? We were going to be a foursome. Dinner. *Arsenic and Old Lace.*"

"That's a great idea," Sharon cried, as much in relief as delight. She had hoped Rosemary would see beneath the foolish façade to the real Billy. Apparently she had.

"He didn't tell you, did he?"

"What's the difference? A foursome will be fun."

Incredibly, Rosemary began to cry. The tears leaked from her eyes as if she were unaware of them and she looked at Sharon tragically.

"Rosemary, cheer up. Billy isn't as bad as all that."

There was a sound on the stairs then and there was Norman, coming downstairs on his hands, his hairy legs waggling in air. Two steps down from the landing, his face purple, he lost his balance. His legs began to churn and then, with a flip, he turned a somersault and landed in a heap at the bottom of the stairs. Sharon applauded with an ironic smile. At least the jerk had gotten dressed. Norman looked up at them, still flushed but pleased with himself.

"Hello, Rosemary."

Well, it was one way to break the ice. Rosemary had stopped crying and Sharon was half convinced when Norman claimed to have broken his leg. But the carpeting was so thick he could have done a swan dive from the landing without risk. She tried to tug him to his feet.

"Rosemary Walsh, this is Norman Sheer."

"Norman, as in conquest. Ten sixty-seven and all that." His brows danced in his Groucho imitation.

"Ten sixty-six," Sharon corrected. "And it's Dr. Sheer, if you can believe it." She kicked him playfully. "Get up in the presence of ladies."

"I usually do."

Sharon crossed her eyes and made a face and led Rosemary through the house and onto the patio in back. Norman took a can of beer from the refrigerator as they passed through the kitchen. Rosemary wanted nothing and neither did Sharon, except maybe some clarity about the big evening Billy had arranged without so much as consulting her. Not that she really resented it. What a nice idea, Rosemary and Billy, Norman and herself. Inside the phone rang and Norman went to answer it.

Absurdly, they sat in silence on the patio, waiting for Norman to come tell them who had called. Billy? Perhaps. Better late than never. But Sharon was suddenly filled with the certainty that they were awaiting bad news. She seemed to have been prepared for this by Rosemary's appearance and inexplicable crying. And then Norman stood in the doorway, an uncharacteristically serious expression on his face.

"I hope that was a joke."

"What is it?" Rosemary's voice was thin and high. Sharon would remember that it was Rosemary who asked, her tone already keyed to what was to come.

"It has to be a joke. Some guy said, 'Mr. Herman was shot at on the golf course and they got Aaron Leib.'"

Sharon just stared at Norman.

"It can't be, Sharon. Imagine your father and Aaron Leib together. Fat chance."

Sharon got to her feet and went into the

kitchen where she picked up the telephone and called the Fox River Country Club and asked to speak to her father. Who was calling? Sharon Herman. That's right. Howard Herman's daughter.

"Just one minute, please."

"I'll bet it was Billy who called," Norman said beside her.

"Don't be an idiot."

"I beg your pardon." Someone was on the line.

Sharon said, "I wasn't talking to you. Who is this?"

It was a policeman named Horvath and he said her father was all right, no harm done.

"Thank God. What happened?"

"Did you hear about it on the radio?"

"Someone called. We thought it was a joke."

"It's no joke. But your father's all right."

"How is Mr. Leib?" she asked, keeping her voice as level as she could. Deep within her another voice demanded hysterically: How is Aaron?

A pause. "Mr. Leib is dead."

Sharon depressed the button, breaking the connection, but continued to hold the phone. She stared at it, a neutral instrument that could be put to such diverse purposes, used to talk with girl friends and boy friends, to make appointments with cosmetic surgeons, to talk with strangers about the death of Aaron Leib and the fact that her father had not been harmed.

The sun still shone but Sharon felt a chill pass over her. A few days ago a shot had been taken at the Israeli consul, and now this. Sharon had grown up with the Holocaust on the edge of her consciousness and the precariousness of the State of Israel was a reminder that no matter what they accomplished, no matter how much they proved themselves with their Einsteins and Freuds and all the rest, there was an irrational hatred just below the surface that could strike out at any time. In a kibbutz on the shores of Lake Galilee she had lived in the knowledge that at any moment all hell could break loose. But it never did, not during the year she was there. Her memories of Israel were of peace, of growing things, of soft green hills and the placid surface of Lake Galilee. And of Aaron Leib.

The violence that had been a constant possibility in Israel had been improbably realized in Fox River. On a golf course.

6

Chuck Howard, special assistant to Congressman Wilfrid Volkser, managed to hustle three first-class seats on the United flight leaving Washington at 8:05 and reaching O'Hare shortly after 9:00 local time, a feat the congressman recognized not at all. It was the nature of Chuck's job to do the impossible and make it look routine. It was the job of all of them in the congressman's office to do the impossible since they had to convince the public their man was a patriotic forward-looking legislator whose sole concern was the commonweal rather than more or less of an obscenity who should get back under his rock.

Chuck tried to get through to Lubins, the administrative assistant, who was in Fox

River, though not in the congressman's district office in the federal building. Nonetheless, he assured Volkser that everything was ready on the home front. Ready for what? Volkser had been thrilled by the news. It is not every day one gets a political assassination in one's own district.

"No, indeed," Chuck said.

"I shall return to Fox River tonight," Volkser announced.

Chuck produced the plane reservations. Volkser said nothing, his mind's eye on some vision of himself descending upon his constituents in this terrible hour.

"I shall return immediately," Volkser murmured, a minor MacArthur.

Except that Volkser was one of the new liberals who sounded an awful lot like old reactionaries. If in the past chauvinism had led to isolationism, it was a professed diffidence about America that led Volkser— and he was not alone—to write off the rest of the world. "Who on earth are we to presume to run the globe?" he would ask in the rumbling tones of his old nemesis, Everett Dirksen. No one was happier than Wilfrid Volkser to see the boys come back from Vietnam, no matter that they had to step lively to get out of there. He had welcomed cutting back in Europe and getting rid of the Panama Canal. "The colonial era is over," he announced, as nation after nation slid into tyranny. "We are only one of the great family of sovereign peoples."

The State of Israel was the *pons asinorum* for Congressman Volkser's vision of the place of America in the world. Tutored by his administrative assistant, Dennis Lubins, he pointed out that those who had been doves when looking westward to the Orient became hawks when their gaze went eastward. He for one had not been returned to Congress from Tel Aviv and he did not propose to let the Knesset call the tune for the Congress of the United States of America. To forestall criticism, he often added remarks critical of the Irish—the IRA, that is, not to be confused with the IRS, the enemy of us all.

This line, while greeted warmly in some quarters and productive of more newspaper coverage than Volkser had ever before enjoyed during fifteen years in Congress, had a negative effect difficult to assess.

Lubins had commissioned two polls,

taken at intervals of four months, and Volkser's popularity in the district was undeniably on the descent. Chuck Howard could have told Volkser that his political survival depended on remaining a largely unknown figure to his constituents, making the office available to those who needed help in the maze of Washington bureaus, doing the indispensable favors, collecting IOU's, and for the love of God resisting the temptation to statesmanship.

"Of course you're right," Lubins said. "Not that it matters."

"He'll listen to you, Denny."

Volkser had been listening to Denny Lubins for the better part of a decade. The trouble was that he was still listening to him. Volkser himself would never have descried in Israel a clear and present danger.

"He's been asked on 'Meet the Press,' Chuck. He'd run naked in the mall before he'd give that up."

"Is he really in trouble in the district?"

Lubins' narrow face became prunelike in thought. "That depends on who runs against him."

"Buford went on the bench," Chuck said. "That leaves Aaron Leib."

Denny nodded. "And Leib is a sonofa-bitch. He's trouble."

"Maybe we should be putting out lines for new employment."

Denny's nose wrinkled. "I'm too old to go straight. Besides, it would give me profound satisfaction to see Aaron Leib beaten by an ass like Volkser. I intend to see that happen."

Lubins' implicit ranking of an as yet undeclared challenger above an incumbent with fifteen years seniority gave Chuck Howard pause. Seven years in Washington had convinced him that a Hire the Handi-capped pennant should fly perpetually over the Capitol. The sobering fact was that Volkser was not so much worse than the majority of his colleagues.

"You shouldn't have sold him on this Israel thing, Denny. 'Meet the Press' or no 'Meet the Press.' "

"It's not that crazy. Haven't you been reading his speeches?"

Meaning Lubins' speeches. Was it possible Denny Lubins believed that drivel? Chuck Howard found this possibility more alarm-ing than the publicity Volkser was getting. There had long been resentment at the arm-twisting on military-aid bills, one gripe led to another, Volkser read a fiery speech on the subject, and before dawn broke over the Virginia hills there was a cohesive little band of neo-isolationists whose chief target was aid to Israel.

It was just Chuck Howard's luck that Lubins should be unreachable in Fox River when the news of the shooting of Aaron Leib came in. This on top of the botched shot in Wrigley Field was impossible to ignore. Ever since the attempt on the Israeli consul, Aaron Leib had been extremely vocal and it seemed generally assumed he was almost certain to run against Wilfrid Volkser. Leib was wealthy and articulate and had a year in which to campaign. The man's death was a golden opportunity for Volkser to weep copious crocodile tears at this cutting down of a promising young man who had been a credit to Fox River and the nation. It was one speech Volkser could be trusted to deliver *a capella*.

The reception at O'Hare was better than Chuck Howard had expected, if less than the congressman thought he deserved. Nor was Volkser whisked away to a waiting skeleton press corps. They were there to meet him in force when he came into the airlines reception area; they moved with him down the long passageway to the main terminal; there were frequent pauses as the nomadic news event was blocked by curious, fascinated travelers. Bright lights, the crush of the inquisitive press and, beyond, the faceless mass of the electorate—Wilfrid Volkser responded to this politician's conception of paradise by spinning off crisp and generally grammatical remarks, neatly balancing his comments on Aaron Leib and the Israeli consul by drawing the moral that this is what happens when nations play fast and loose with the sovereignty of other states. Was this aimed at the presumed origins of the assassin or was it an I-told-you-so directed at Jerusalem?

"Gentlemen, I do not propose to anticipate the results of the investigation now being vigorously pursued. At the moment my thoughts are on the victim and his bereaved family."

"Who will replace Leib as your opponent in the next election, Congressman?"

Volkser frowned. "That is a crude question betraying a crude cast of mind."

Though other questions bubbled forth,

Volkser held up a huge hand. The interview was over. He was on his way to express condolences to the widow.

"Where the hell is Lubins?" Volkser asked out of the corner of a mouth that yet retained its smile.

"Damned if I know."

"Get me out of here. I thought you said Lubins would meet us."

Chuck Howard had said nothing of the kind. In the car, Volkser continued to bitch about Lubins. It was a sign of his pleasure. Good luck always convinced him he didn't really need Dennis Lubins.

"I've seen even less of him since he got rid of his wife."

The suggestion that his staff must be eunuchs for the kingdom of Volkser's sake was not a welcome one to Chuck Howard. But he found himself wondering if Volkser knew something he didn't. Had Lubins come back to Fox River in the hope of reconciling with Gladys? He shivered. How could anyone prefer wedlock to the fox-in-the-chicken-coop existence of the unattached male in the nation's capital? And wedlock to Gladys, the nutcracker sweet, at that?

7

Roger Dowling decided to walk to Rosemary's apartment, which was four long and two short blocks from St. Hilary's rectory.

The summer evening was warm and the sound of the traffic on the Interstate that formed one side of the triangle in which his parish fell came to Father Dowling almost as a reassurance. The pell-mell race went on, suburbanites hurtling homeward from hectic days in the city or tourists by-passing Chicago as quickly as they could. This Euclidean piece of Fox River, cut off from the rest, particularly from the new and growing portions of the city, seemed to have preserved Fox River as it had been. St. Hilary's was no plum in the estimation of the powers in the chancery office, and they were right if plumhood be gauged by the promise of growth, expansion, busyness.

On the sidewalk before him was a fading pattern of chalked squares. Hopscotch. Was it an illusion that there were more kids in the neighborhood than a year ago? Maybe St. Hilary's would enjoy a second spring and confound them all. The parish school could be returned to its original use, if it came to that. It served now as a parish center, catering to the retired, to mothers of children, to the unemployed. It was a pleasant thought, the school jammed with kids, their voices in the playground during recess, Roger Dowling wandering among them. A dream. An unlikely dream. St. Hilary's would continue its dignified descent and in the meantime he would minister to the survivors whose demands on him were the traditional ones. He found it difficult not to adjust his step to the pattern of the chalked hopscotch game.

A gray squirrel darted across the walk and sprang at a tree, clinging momentarily before climbing it like the stripe on a barber pole. The adaptability of the rodent. Had that animal's ancestors lived in some forest primeval? The present generation of squirrels, like the present generation of men, had to make do in a world of concrete and macadam with the vegetation necessary for survival sending its roots deep beneath the surface encrustations. Roger Dowling hoped these hardy trees offset at least in part the noxious fumes wafted from the Interstate.

Rosemary lived in a small four-unit apartment building that occupied almost to its edges a lot in the middle of the block. There was an abbreviated lawn in front of the building and, by and large, it fitted in with the houses flanking it. Inside the front door, Roger Dowling pressed the button over Rosemary's mail box. Hers was not identified as were the others. Schmidt. Hanson. Blyleven. And blank. Blank for Rosemary.

There was the sound of ascending feet and a door at the end of the vestibule opened. An elderly man in overalls, carrying a large push broom, emerged. He seemed unaware of the priest's presence.

"Good evening," Father Dowling said.

The man did not answer. Deaf, or perhaps anticlerical. But then he turned his head, saw Roger Dowling, and stepped back, raising the broom as if to defend himself.

"Good evening," Father Dowling repeated.

The man seemed to watch his lips. "Oh, yeah. Hello, Reverend. You scared me."

Roger Dowling pressed Rosemary's bell again. "Have you seen Miss Walsh?"

"She won't put a name over her mail box."

"I'm sorry I frightened you. You haven't seen Miss Walsh?"

"When would I see anyone?" the old man asked ruefully. "Living down there in the basement."

"My name is Roger Dowling. I'm the pastor at Saint Hilary's."

"People think it's a good deal, rent-free apartment and all that. They don't know what it's like. Too many trees in the neighborhood. And squirrels. They're hell on a roof." He squinted devilishly at Father Dowling as if he expected an objection to his salty language.

"Do you live alone?"

"I'm a widower. Twice."

He said this proudly, as if he expected congratulations. Well, it was a feat of sorts for a man to outlive two wives, though apparently it was a mixed blessing. Roger Dowling could imagine the loneliness. But it

72

had been the man's fear that bothered him more.

"What's your name?"

"Wilson. Woodward Wilson. Call me Woodie." He grinned, displaying an absence of teeth. "My second wife objected to people calling me Woodie. Don't ask me why. She called me Ward."

"Miss Walsh doesn't seem to be in."

"Never see her. Must be quiet. Of course, living in the basement..."

He went on again about the disadvantages of his basement apartment and Roger Dowling was struck by the man's frailty. Rosemary should have a more vigorous and alert caretaker than this. He pressed the bell a third time, convinced now it was pointless.

Wilson came outside with him, dropped his broom with a plunk, and began listlessly to raise dust from the sidewalk with it. Roger Dowling looked up at the windows of Rosemary's apartment, afire with the setting sun. Wilson talked to himself as he pushed the broom the length of the short walk. He stopped, leaned on the broom handle, and surveyed the street.

"There's one of the damned things now."

He lifted the broom to indicate a squirrel

whose head appeared around the bole of a tree between sidewalk and curb. Making a mock rifle of his broom, Wilson whispered, "Pow." He turned to Dowling, wearing again his devilish grin.

"Fellow told me I should get a BB gun and let the little beggars know who's boss."

"They're pretty quick."

"So'm I," Wilson bragged, but not even he could believe that. "They shot some guy on a golf course a little while ago. Heard it on the news."

Roger Dowling did not want to discuss the slaying of Aaron Leib with Mr. Wilson. But neither did he want to leave.

"The Cubs lost today," he said.

"Man bites dog."

"I don't follow you."

"It's not news. They always lose."

"Not always."

Wilson snorted. "I'm a Sox fan."

Roger Dowling felt surprise. He would have thought Wilson would be attracted by the persistent failure he attributed, not without foundation, to the Cubs. An American League fan was an unfathomable mystery in any case.

"Do you play cribbage or checkers, Mr. Wilson?"

The old man looked at him. "Right now I've got to sweep this walk."

"I didn't mean now. Do you know where Saint Hilary's is? We've turned the school into a parish center. Folks come by there to talk, play cards, that sort of thing. You're welcome to come."

"I'm not Catholic."

"Not everyone who comes is. It's a social center."

"Never was one for church going, not even with my first wife. She was the one, Reverend. Twice on Sundays, at least once during the week." Wilson shook his head.

"What denomination was she?"

"She wasn't. She was a Baptist."

"I mean it about the center."

"Maybe I will. Well..."

Wilson gave his broom a shove. Roger Dowling felt like a salesman who has failed to make a sale. He would have liked to dally longer in the hope Rosemary would come, unable to rid himself of his fear for her. Reluctantly he said good-by to Mr. Wilson.

When he was not yet to the corner he turned to see that Mr. Wilson was no longer outside. As if he had already decided to do this, Roger Dowling walked quickly back to the building and inside. He went upstairs to the door of Rosemary's apartment, slipped a credit card between the frame and door, and pushed. It opened easily, too easily, and that seemed to justify his decision to go inside and wait until Rosemary returned.

8

In the confusion at the Hermans, Rosemary slipped away. She told herself she was neither wanted nor needed, but the fear that had sent her there returned with the arrival of Mrs. Herman, as if Sharon's mother brought with her the threat of Anne and Archy.

The thought that the band she had deserted was operating in Fox River made a mockery of her effort to become anonymous and she could half believe that the shooting at the ball park and now the killing of Aaron Leib were meant as signals to her. They had found her, they were reminding her of their mode of action. She had known there were no provisions for leaving the band, alive. To be one of them was to turn her back forever on the ordinary life she was trying to live again. They could not permit her to return to that.

When the news of the shooting on the golf course of the Fox River Country Club crackled over the radio, Rosemary had run into Gladys's office to hear it. Gladys was not there. No one else was in the office. Gladys always left her radio on. At the window, Rosemary looked out back and was startled to see that her car was gone. That was when she decided to flee.

Now, Rosemary walked along the wide curving suburban street, unsure of directions, wanting simply to move. There seemed little chance of finding a cab here and she did not know where she might find a bus stop. The luxurious houses, set back on huge lots with plush lawns and carefully tended shrubs and garden beds, seemed a metaphor of peace, a peace she had tried unsuccessfully to rediscover. Just such a suburban peace had been violated on the country club golf course.

The sun had set, but twilight lingered. A dog barked, there was the sound of children at play, romping in a pool invisible behind a high hedge. Rosemary walked at least a mile before she came to a small shopping center. In a drugstore, she had to wait to use the phone. The pharmacist had a radio on and it was there that she heard of the phone call from Anne and Archy claiming credit for the killing of Leib. That her guess had been right did little to lessen her dread. She had never doubted they were behind it, not after the shot at Wrigley Field two days before.

After she had phoned for a cab, she waited inside the store until she saw the taxi enter the parking lot and cruise slowly, its driver on the lookout for his fare. When he neared the drugstore, Rosemary dashed out and climbed in.

"You the one who called?"

"Yes."

He continued to look back at her. "Where you want to go?"

Without thinking, she gave him her home address. Immediately the car gathered speed. Did she want to go home? Did she dare? No alternative came to her and she settled back in the seat. Where was she safe if they had indeed found her? Work? She leaned forward and told the driver of her change of destination. His eyes studied her in the rearview mirror. He shrugged.

Women, his manner seemed to say.

Her car was not in the parking lot behind the realty office.

She had let the cab go, entered the office where the sound of Gladys's radio created the illusion that the place was not empty. She went into Gladys's office. No one. She turned off the radio and went to the window to make certain her car was gone. It was gone. Gladys, from whom she had bought the car, had kept an extra set of keys under the floor mat and Rosemary had continued the practice. How dumb that seemed now, except that car thieves do not need keys. The extra set was protection against her own forgetfulness, not against theft. She did not doubt her car had been stolen.

She stepped back from the window, fearful someone might still be out there, observing her. The movement had the effect of calming her. She felt a surprisng return of the cool confidence that had once been hers, fear shuffled off by the attitude with which she had worked with the band. Step one consisted in dismissing the fear of death. Death was to be expected, eventually; it could be welcomed if encountered while doing what had to be done. One could not expect to fight society without society striking back. "We are already dead," Archy had said. "We have died to it all. They can't take anything from us we haven't already given up voluntarily." Memories of that training gave Rosemary an almost carefree confidence. Where would they look for her? Her apartment? But she imagined them discounting that. They would assume that once she was aware of their presence in Fox River she would never return to her apartment. So she went to her apartment.

But not directly. From the bus stop, she walked to St. Hilary's rectory. Father Dowling was the only person with whom she could discuss what was happening.

"He's not in, Miss," the housekeeper said, standing in the doorway as if she were guarding the house.

"Do you expect him back?"

"I don't know when it will be. Did you want to wait?"

"No. No, thank you."

Rosemary turned away and her legs were leaden as she walked out to the street. She felt as if a last slim hope had gone. A block from the rectory, involuntarily, she skipped through the squares of a hopscotch game.

Inside her building, she opened the basement door and went downstairs. The roar of the TV behind Mr. Wilson's door made the panels vibrate. She knocked, doubting he would be able to hear her against the broadcast sirens and squealing tires of the program he was watching. She turned the knob and pushed the door open. Mr. Wilson sat in an overstuffed chair, his head back, his mouth open, sound asleep. Rosemary tugged his sleeve. His mouth closed and made smacking noises but he did not wake up. Rosemary shook him by the shoulder and his old eyes popped open and tried to focus on her.

"Mr. Wilson."

"What is it? What do you want?"

"I'm sorry to wake you."

He grumbled as if to deny that he had been asleep. "He find you?"

"Was someone here for me?"

She could not hear his answer.

"Do you mind?" She turned down the volume of the television. "Mr. Wilson." She paused, looking down at the frail little man. If she fled again, would she be leaving this old man to the mercy of those who had no mercy? But again she felt an icy calmness.

"Mr. Wilson, could you come upstairs and look at my kitchen sink?"

"Now?"

"Please. I'd really appreciate it."

"What seems to be wrong?"

"I'm not sure."

"Does it clog or what?"

"Can you fix it?"

He struggled out of his chair. "I'll get my tools."

"Oh, good. Look, I'll run ahead. Can you just let yourself in the back door?"

"Fine. Fine."

She left his room, pulling the door shut behind her. The basement was dimly visible when she turned. A huge furnace occupied its center, its fat pipes reaching like so many arms into the deeper gloom. Rosemary went behind the furnace and waited, closing her eyes to pray she was not putting the old man in danger. She was doing this to protect him.

In a minute the door opened again and Mr. Wilson came out carrying a toolbox. He muttered to himself as he started up the stairs. The lobby door opened and closed. Rosemary waited thirty seconds before following. On the second floor, she saw the old figure of Mr. Wilson moving slowly down the corridor to the far end and her kitchen door. She pressed back and waited. The toolbox made a clink when Mr. Wilson set it down. She heard the scratch of his key.

When Rosemary stepped to her front door, she had her key in hand. She put her ear to the panel. She heard the kitchen door open, but there was no sound from within her apartment. She counted to three, put her key in the lock, twisted it, pushed, and burst into her apartment. With a single move she was at the fireplace where she snatched up the poker and turned.

The poker rose menacingly in her hand as she wheeled toward the kitchen.

She stopped.

Father Dowling, halfway to the kitchen, turned and stared at her with wide startled eyes.

9

Mrs. Patricia Leib, a handsome woman in her mid-thirties, received Captain Keegan after a small delay. She sat in her living room, in the center of a couch, holding a handkerchief. The handkerchief was neatly folded and showed no signs of use, nor did her eyes seem those of a woman who, upon learning she had just become a widow, burst into tears. But, if he was judging her, Phil Keegan felt that he too was being silently assessed.

"I'm very sorry to be here under these circumstances, Mrs. Leib."

"Surely you're not surprised." Her tone was accusing.

"How do you mean?"

"The first time they missed. This

time they didn't."

"You're referring to the terrorists? The Anne and Archy band?"

"Of course. They've taken 'credit' for it, haven't they?"

"Yes."

"Just as they did after the incident at the ball park."

"Had your husband received any threats?"

She laughed as if she were beading the sounds on a thread of time, pearly note after pearly note. "Private threats? Of course not. Isn't the whole point that they should be public, a news event? Aaron's life has been in danger ever since he dedicated himself to the cause of Israel."

"Tell me about that."

"It's hardly a secret, Captain. Aaron was not exactly shy about what he was doing." She paused. "I warned him, Captain. After the shooting at the ball game. I told him he should shut up for awhile and stop drawing attention to himself." She placed the handkerchief on her knees and ran a smoothing hand over it several times. Her eyes lifted to engage Keegan's. "Aaron was convinced the Israeli consul was the target."

"That was a reasonable assumption."

"It may have been reasonable, but it was wrong."

Keegan was relieved that she was not hysterical, but her calmness began to bother him almost as much as weeping would have.

"I don't suppose you're equipped to handle a thing of this magnitude, are you, Captain?"

"How do you mean?"

"Won't it require outside help? National? International?"

Keegan thought of the trio he had just left in Robertson's office. The Fox River Chief of Police had been visibly exhilarated at having seated across his desk representatives of the FBI and CIA as well as an assistant chief from Chicago. Robertson had instructed Keegan to make available to these gentlemen everything they had on Aaron Leib. Keegan could see in Threpplewaite's eyes that the CIA man doubted the Fox River police had anything he did not already have. No doubt they became interested in people like Leib who threw themselves headlong into international affairs.

"Aaron Leib might very well have been elected to represent this district in Congress," Robertson said confidingly. He seemed determined to alert his visitors to everything they could find in the newspapers.

"Have you talked to the widow?" Threpplewaite asked Keegan.

"I was on my way there."

Threpplewaite's expression was enigmatic and, remembering it in the Leib living room, Keegan wondered if the CIA man had been trying to tell him something. At the time he had countered by asking Threpplewaite and the man from the FBI, Franks, what they were doing about Anne and Archy.

Franks made a gesture. "We know about them, of course. We know a lot and a little. To tell you the truth, we had thought they'd faded away."

"They've been inactive."

"For over a year. Most of these groups are disbanding now."

"Times are changing," Robertson said, and silence formed in ripples about this platitudinous pebble.

Now Keegan asked Patricia Leib, "Did your husband have local enemies?"

"Of course."

"Why of course?"

"A man like Aaron Leib makes enemies

the way other men make footprints. He was a very determined person. While he was in business and since. Not everyone will weep because he is gone."

Looking at Leib's dry-eyed widow smoothing an unused handkerchief on her knee, Phil Keegan could not help thinking she was speaking of herself as well. But there seemed no acceptable way he could ask this new widow why she did not weep. He would have liked to admire her courage, her stoicism, but he could not. He himself had cried helplessly when his wife died and he had been in no state to talk to anyone for hours after it happened.

"Had you been aware of his plans to golf with Howard Herman?"

She smiled very slightly and shook her head.

"Was Herman a friend of his?"

"Perhaps. I've heard the name but I don't believe I have ever met Howard Herman."

"He is a member of the country club."

"I don't golf, Captain."

"Do you go to the club?"

"Very seldom."

"When did you learn your husband would

be golfing with Howard Herman this afternoon?"

"I learned they were golfing together when I heard what had happened to Aaron. I didn't know it in advance. My husband and I did not synchronize our schedules, Captain."

"Are there children?"

Again the wintry smile. She shook her head slowly as if she knew he already knew the answer to the question.

"Tell me, Captain. Why have you come here?"

"I should think that's obvious. Your husband has been murdered."

The word did not shake her. "Yes. By a terrorist band. Their motives are, I should think, obvious. Nothing I can tell you would possibly aid the agencies that will be inquiring into this. Not that I expect them to find the killer."

"Why not?" He did not like the suggestion that he was interfering.

"Do they ever, in cases like this?"

This angered Keegan, and he was still angry when he left, a reaction he tried unsuccessfully to feel ashamed of while he drove to St. Hilary's rectory. He had the irrational desire to dazzle Mrs. Leib with the speed and efficiency with which her husband's murderer would be found, but this desire, alas, amounted to little more than the hope that investigations other than his own might succeed. In Washington, in Chicago, throughout the country and the world, the search would go on with resources infinitely beyond those he could command. But still he stubbornly hoped that all the fancy and clandestine agencies in the world would fail and he would succeed in finding the one responsible for Aaron Leib's death on a golf course in Fox River.

"And that's the point, Roger," he said, comfortable in the rectory study, a bottle of beer sweating in his hand. "The man was killed right here. The body is here. It's a local matter. I don't give a damn about the international ramifications."

"Anne and Archy?"

"I hate that name."

"I don't suppose there's any doubt that terrorists are responsible for Aaron Leib's death?"

Keegan only frowned and sipped his beer.

"Was the same weapon used, Phil?"

Leave it to Roger to get down to details.

The trouble was, there was no answer to his question. The slug dug out of the woodwork in Wrigley Field had been so beaten up it would be hard to match with a weapon. If they had a weapon.

"And we still haven't found the slug that killed Leib."

"Well, there's the phone call."

"Sure there is. And you or I could make a phone call, claiming to have killed Leib. As a matter of fact, we've had competing claims. Obvious nuts, of course, but even so."

Roger Dowling nodded. "If we were impressionable or unbalanced, having heard of the phone call after the ball park attempt, we could call now and say we were Anne and Archy?"

The trouble with having it out in the open, expressed, was that it seemed a ridiculous idea, one he could cling to only for childish reasons, to impress the big shots. And Mrs. Leib. But it *was* the ordinary thing to receive phone calls after a sensational crime, a kidnaping, a murder, the loonies coming out from their holes to confess. And they did confess, to things they could not possibly have done. They seemed to crave even a brief opprobrium. Was a phone call alone enough to slake the thirst for imagined iniquity? He told Roger Dowling of Mrs. Leib's remark that not everyone in Fox River would be sorry her husband was dead.

"Could she have meant him?" Roger indicated the screen of the TV where Congressman Wilfrid Volkser's arrival at O'Hare was being shown on the late news.

"Leib hadn't announced his candidacy, Roger."

"Wouldn't that have been only a formality?"

"Perhaps. But Volkser can't really be happy about this. For one thing, the immediate effect should be a rise in sympathy for Israel. I mean, people are going to ask, what is this? Shooting at Israeli consuls, killing a man who raised all kinds of money for Israel? The indignation isn't going to help Volkser stop that military-aid bill. And if he's defeated in that attempt, an opponent far less attractive than Aaron Leib will be able to give him a run for his money."

"That's interesting."

"Now, if I were looking for explanations

of Leib's murder..."

"If!"

"I mean, if we hadn't any idea who'd done it..."

"It's not like you to accept a ready-made solution, Phil."

Keegan looked at his old friend. He enjoyed these unbuttoned chats with Roger Dowling about current police work. They were more helpful than he would have liked to admit to anyone other than Roger himself. Keegan had often been surprised by the priest's ability to see through a forest of facts to the essential truth of guilt or innocence. Or both. Roger Dowling saw things from an odd perspective. Of course he had to, being a priest, Keegan understood that. Sometimes he actually derived comfort that there was that different outlook around. As for himself, he figured that once you nailed somebody with a crime, you threw the book at him and no mistake. How the hell could society function otherwise? Still and all, a criminal remained a man and it was good to know there were those like Roger Dowling who never lost sight of the fact.

"You like the far-out solution, Roger. But

sometimes, even in crime, things are really what they seem."

Which was true. He repeated it to himself on the way home. But among the things that seemed, and therefore were, was a widow neither surprised nor particularly upset by her husband's death, and not all the terrorist bands in the world were a sufficient explanation of that.

"Leib got around with other women," Horvath said on the phone. Back in his apartment, Keegan had brewed a cup of instant coffee preparatory to turning in, and decided to give Cy a call.

"Is that just talk, or did you get names?"

"I got one name."

"Tell me."

"Gladys Lubins. She's a realtor who sold Leib the house he lives in. Apparently he sold her a thing or two as well."

"Is she single?"

"Divorced. Apparently he entertained her at the country club a couple of times. Word got back to his wife."

"Who told you this?"

"Several people. A man named Bernstein, for one. He says Mrs. Leib gave her husband a big 'Or else' and he stopped seeing the Lubins woman. But there were others too. Usually he was more discreet."

Keegan had a hunch about such reputations. One discovered affair and the miscreant was assumed to be guilty of dozens of undiscovered ones. He said, "I would have thought Leib was too busy to be a playboy."

"There are people who wish he'd spent more time being a playboy. I gather he was a real pest raising money for Israel. The implication that he was the only one who really cared ticked off a lot of people. And he had a way of shaming them into giving more than they could afford."

"Hmmm."

"Any word from the FBI?"

Again Keegan bristled. "We can't depend on them to fry our fish for us, Cy. We'll just carry on with our investigation."

"Right."

And it was right. It had nothing to do with Roger Dowling or with Mrs. Leib either. It had a helluva lot more to do with the annoyance it would cause Robertson, who doubtless viewed the local investigation as interference with the FBI and CIA.

"Not to mention Israeli Intelligence," Horvath said.

"Why do you say that?"

"Doesn't it figure?"

10

If Father Dowling had had any doubt that Rosemary Walsh was worried by the apparent operation of Anne and Archy in Chicago and Fox River, the sight of her advancing on him with a raised poker would have dispelled it.

"Father Dowling!" she cried, stopping.

"Fear not, Rosemary. It is I." A stilted speech, perhaps, even presumptuous, but at the moment he did feel somewhat like Our Lord advancing across the water to Simon Peter.

"Hey, what's going on?" Wilson asked, shuffling in from the kitchen. Rosemary still held the poker as if ready to strike.

"This is Father Dowling," Rosemary said, letting her hand drop. There was a quaver in her voice that might have portended hysterical laughter.

"I know. We met. What are you doing with the poker?"

"Have you looked at the sink?"

"Ain't nothing wrong with your sink."

"Are you sure?"

Rosemary guided the old man back to the kitchen, handing the poker to Father Dowling as she passed him. The priest listened in wonderment as she talked, ran water, and urged Wilson to find something wrong with the kitchen sink, doubtless hoping that thereby the odd tableau the building superintendent had come upon would fade from his mind.

"Isn't that the funniest thing," Rosemary said. "It's perfectly all right now."

"That's what I said."

"Thank you so much for looking at it, Mr. Wilson."

"I told you to call me Woodie."

"Woodie. Thank you. I don't know what I'd do without you."

She let him out the back door, sweet-talking until the latch clicked. Wearing a resigned expression, she came back into the living room.

"Did Mr. Wilson let you in, Father?"

"Oh, no." He showed her the credit card he had used.

She laughed. "You broke in!"

"Rosemary, you can't stay here."

She dropped into a chair and her arms fell to her sides. "My car is missing."

"Where have you been?"

Her account of dashing out of the office and taking a cab to the Hermans, the arrival of Mrs. Herman, her trip back to the office where she verified that her car was missing, her visit to the rectory, was so charmingly confused that for a moment Roger Dowling felt as bewildered as poor Wilson had been.

"Was your car there when you went to the Hermans?"

"No. I looked. It was gone."

"Who else was in the office?"

"No one."

"Had there been?"

"Oh, yes."

"Did anyone there ever use your car?"

"Once I let Mr. Baxter use it, but no one would take it without asking."

"Someone did, Rosemary."

"I mean, no one in the office."

"Of course they wouldn't have a key, would they?"

She told him of the key under the floor mat. He could imagine it lying there. How many other people made use of the same "hiding place"? And what earthly good was such a key if she mistakenly locked it in the car? Father Dowling stood.

"First thing, you have to eat."

"Eat? I'm not hungry."

"Well, I am and Mrs. Murkin will be very impatient. Come on. I'm inviting you."

Mrs. Murkin was impatient and not a little surprised to find that Father Dowling had invited Rosemary Walsh to dine with him. The housekeeper served them briskly and in silence, her expression injured and aloof. Rosemary discovered that she did indeed have an appetite and her praise of Mrs. Murkins' cooking broke the older woman's silence. Afterward, Rosemary insisted on helping with the dishes and Father Dowling could hear the two women chattering happily in the kitchen. Mrs. Murkin was in a receptive mood when Father Dowling went in to them and said that Rosemary would have to spend the night in the rectory.

"Father, I can go to a motel."

"No. What arrangements can we make, Marie?"

"She's staying here?"

"It's important," Father Dowling said, and Mrs. Murkin did not mistake the tone of his voice.

"Why, it's no problem at all. She can use my room and I'll sleep on the couch in the sewing room."

"I'm not staying," Rosemary said.

"The couch opens into a bed," Mrs. Murkin explained. "Come, I'll show you."

"Father, please."

But he did not restrain Mrs. Murkin from taking the girl into the little room that opened off the kitchen. Mrs. Murkin told Rosemary she would need her help in getting the couch pulled out anyway. And so it was settled.

"Just for tonight," Rosemary said, before going up the back stairs to Mrs. Murkins' bedroom.

"Certainly for tonight," Father Dowling replied.

The two women went upstairs together, Mrs. Murkin wanting to show her guest where things were. Ten minutes later the housekeeper came into Roger Dowling's study.

"Is she all settled down?"

"Yes." Mrs. Murkin was waiting for an explanation.

"I'm worried about her safety, Marie."

"Well, she'll be safe enough here."

"I can't give you details."

"Have I asked for details?"

"Good."

"Do you want anything?"

"Is there any beer?"

She lifted her brows. She knew Father Dowling did not drink. "Yes, there is beer."

"Phil Keegan may drop by."

He watched her put two and two together and did not prevent her from arriving at the wrong sum. It did no harm for Mrs. Murkin to think their ward's safety was a concern of Captain Philip Keegan.

"I could make popcorn, Father."

He assured her that wasn't necessary. He wasn't sure when Phil Keegan would arrive, if at all. Mystified but placated, Marie Murkin went off to her makeshift bed.

So it was that, while Father Dowling and Phil Keegan spoke, Rosemary Walsh was ensconced in the housekeeper's bedroom.

Father Dowling himself went into the kitchen to fetch Phil Keegan's beer lest the closed door of the sewing room excite the interest of the detective. That fear was a mild one, of course. Phil Keegan was perfectly content to sprawl in the study and accept the beer brought to him.

It was with Rosemary in mind that Father Dowling had gently urged his old friend to see the killing of Aaron Leib as he would have without the earlier shooting in Cub Park. Phil Keegan was rightly jealous of the territory of his own obligations, and, until Leib's murder was shown to be anything other than a local matter, it should not be delivered over to outsiders.

Much later, in his room upstairs, reading in bed, Father Dowling's thoughts turned to Rosemary's missing automobile. He prayed it would turn out that one of the salesmen had borrowed it on the spur of the moment without telling Rosemary. For all either of them knew, it was even now back where it belonged, parked behind Fox River Realty. But, having turned off the light, he commented on his own prayer by whistling briefly in the dark.

11

It was only a month after he was let out of Joliet that Lennie Miller's parole officer got him the job with Childers as driver, messenger, factotum.

"Fac what?" Lennie was smoking without pleasure the filtertip O'Boyle had given him. The parole officer had pushed the pack across his messy desk, maneuvering it between mounds of paper, scattered letters, junk.

"Jack-of-all-trades," O'Boyle said, tugging at his beard apologetically.

Lennie did not really understand O'Boyle, but he was familiar with the type. O'Boyle acted as if society was getting one more chance to do its duty by Lennie Miller. It was an old con's theory: society—the power structure—was the real villain. If Lennie had sometimes sung that song himself, he had never believed it, and he assumed no one else at Joliet did either. But O'Boyle believed it. That eyebrow-knitted sincerity of his could not be faked. Oh, how the probation officer had lapped up the story of Lennie's early life, nodding enthusiastically through the tale as if he could have told it himself. The shiftless father and the harassed mother who drank too much, but who could blame her? A bum school, rotten neighborhood, bad companions—what else could Lennie have become but what he was? Well, he might have turned out like his brother or both his sisters, but on O'Boyle's theory *they* were the freaks, not Lennie.

"Who is Childers, Mr. O'Boyle?"

"He is a prominent Fox River business consultant."

Whatever the hell that was. "Does he know who I've driven before?"

"You just keep your nose clean and show Childers you deserve his trust and everything will be fine."

"Tell me what a business consultant is."

O'Boyle didn't know, exactly. The doings of the straight world were more of a mystery to him than they were to Lennie Miller. Except that Childers was not exactly straight. On one later visit to O'Boyle, Lennie had hinted as much, but the probation officer didn't pick it up.

"How much do you make, O'Boyle?"

"Do you think I'm in this for the money?"

"Just for the satisfaction?"

"You could say that."

Satisfaction, a shirt pocket full of leaky ball-point pens, and a messy desk. "You should have been a priest."

O'Boyle laughed. "Half the priests I know envy me my job."

"You're kidding."

"I'm doing something real here, Lennie. Look at yourself. Who would have thought a couple months ago you'd be living as you now are?"

"You got a point."

His life was a pimp's life. Well, not quite. Childers got his own women, but he sent Lennie to pick them up and drop them off at the apartment in Chicago. The guy was as careful as a minister on the town. He was never seen in public with any of those girls. He arrived alone and he left alone, using public transportation, and, if he took a cab, he got out a block or two from the apartment, and never at the same corner, either. The guy was almost pathological about his respectability. He got mad as hell the time Lennie offered to put him on to some good stuff, a redhead. Even to his own driver, he couldn't admit what the apartment was for and why the girls were brought there. Did he think they wouldn't talk to Lennie?

"You just a chauffeur or what?" Rita had asked him the first time.

Lennie tipped back his head and laughed, the way Childers did. "Sure," he said. "Just a chauffeur." He could see in the rearview mirror that she accepted this ironic disclaimer.

"How about you and me getting together, Rita?"

"I don't know. Where?"

"The apartment is a business expense Lionel and I share."

"Lionel?"

"Childers."

"Is that his name?"

"Couldn't you tell?"

Rita giggled and he guessed, rightly, that they could have a lot of fun talking about what she and Childers did in the apartment.

"You're sure different, Lennie. That's why I thought..."

"That I was a chauffeur? Forget it. No offense taken."

So he got together with Rita, but they hadn't used the apartment. She hated the place and, once she started blabbing, Lennie didn't blame her. Who would have thought it of old Lionel? Besides, Lennie figured it would be best if Childers had less chance of finding out about his poaching. So they went to Rita's place.

She was a funny bird, plush where she ought to be, but she still gave the impression of being a spindly kid, which is what she had been before her breasts bloomed and her hips widened and her career began at the age of fifteen. Lennie could get a kick out of just lying there beside her and exchanging stories about their childhoods.

"What do you really do, Lennie? For Childers?"

"I'm his driver."

"Come on."

"No, it's true."

He told her about Joliet too, but he made sure she understood he had brains; he knew his IQ and was not reluctant to mention it, not that Rita knew what the figure meant. "I'm a genius," he told her, stretching the point. Actually about thirty-five points.

She was diddling around with his chest and one of her nails was broken but he didn't complain. Sometimes, in the dark, he told himself he loved her, but of course he knew you don't fall in love with hookers. You don't really trust them either, no matter how sympathetic they were. Call Rita a pal, then. She was a great pal. And she never did quite believe that all he was was a driver.

Childers never forgot Lennie's status, that's for sure. And he was curious about Joliet, asking what it had been like.

"You wouldn't like it," Lennie told him, and for a spooky moment he wasn't sure Childers would take it as a joke.

"You must have met some weird types there."

"It's like anywhere else."

"You think the world is full of crooks and murderers?"

Lennie certainly thought Childers was something else than the representative of business virtue O'Boyle took him to be. Childers was consulted by businesses having unusual problems—problems with hijacking, espionage, mysterious losses. It soon occurred to Lennie that if Childers had something to do with creating these problems, it would make solving them a lot easier.

"I have had a peculiar inquiry," Childers said when the Big Subject had been introduced. Lennie sensed something was up, but said nothing. "I have a client who is interested in getting rid of someone."

"Uh huh."

"There are men who take on jobs like that, aren't there?"

"I suppose."

"Of course the fee would have to be attractive."

"It sure would."

"Ten thousand dollars?"

Lennie whistled.

"Could you, using extreme discretion, make inquiries among your former friends?"

"That's dangerous, Mr. Childers. Just talking about it is dangerous. Especially for a guy with my record."

Childers nodded. "I've come to trust you, Lennie."

"I'll think about it."

He thought about it a lot. After a while,

he seemed to think about nothing else. Ten thou. He thought of cutting the offer in half, providing a commission for himself. And then he began to wonder why he should split it at all. There was a way to keep the whole nut. There was one sure way.

12

Lionel Childers licked the succulent syrup from his spoon and seriously considered ordering another chocolate sundae. He loved sweets. He kept a five-pound box of chocolates in his office and offered them like cigars to visitors, but he always ended by eating the lion's share himself.

"I wish I dared," Billy Herman said. Billy had lunched on a salad consisting of little more than cottage cheese and a slice of pineapple, while Childers had feasted on lasagna, a mixed salad heavy with thousand-island dressing, and now a chocolate sundae. "Not that I have any appetite," Billy added.

"How is your father doing?"

"They sedated him pretty heavily. So he could sleep."

"A harrowing experience."

Lionel Childers had dropped by the Herman house the morning after the dreadful event on the fifteenth hole of the country club golf course. Mrs. Herman had not remembered him but she did not resist when he enveloped her in his arms and murmured words of consolation. Billy appeared behind his mother and, visibly surprised to see his father's business associate in his home, made the introductions.

"A business associate?" Mrs. Herman asked.

"Mr. Childers is a business consultant," Billy said.

"We can be grateful the gunman missed your husband," Childers said. "Have you spoken with Mrs. Leib?"

"I don't even know the woman."

"Ah well, at a time like this..."

The suggestion put Mrs. Herman on the defensive, as if she were guilty of some social gaffe. Unlike the compassionate Lionel Childers. He was only there to show the flag, of course. It did no harm to remind a client of services rendered. Howard Herman, heavily sedated, was still in bed.

"I'm sorry to hear that," Childers said.

"That is, I am sorry I cannot tell him personally how relieved I was to learn he had survived that cowardly attack."

"You may be sure I'll tell him you called, Mr. . . . ."

"Childers. Lionel Childers."

"Thanks," Billy said. He seemed a harmless young man in his mother's presence.

"Come along, Billy," Childers said. "I'll buy you lunch."

And so he had, if a mess of cottage cheese can be called lunch.

"I think I'll have another of these, Billy. Could I interest you in joining me?"

Billy had watched hungrily as Childers consumed the first chocolate sundae, and the prospect of witnessing another such catering to the inner man obviously demoralized him. On the other hand, Billy's self-denial could suggest a man in control of his passions, guided by his head rather than his stomach. But Childers resisted this estimate of his luncheon companion. Armies, he assured himself, travel on their stomachs. Generals certainly do, whatever might be said of snipers.

"You needn't stay, Billy. I know you must have things to do."

"Yes." For a moment Billy's eyes were steely, and then he pushed away from the table. Childers watched young Herman wander away among the tables, his melancholy gaze falling on the plates of the diners. All Billy talked of when the topic of food arose was calories. Calories! Childers dismissed such nonsense with contempt; but then, he was blessed with a metabolism that enabled him to eat like Gargantua and look like Savonarola.

When his second chocolate sundae came, Lionel Childers savored it slowly and thought of Fox River Casing, whose sedated president now slept the sleep of the just.

Howard Herman had first consulted Lionel Childers when a truckload of steel, delivery of which he had accepted when it was loaded on the truck in Gary, failed to reach Fox River Casing. Childers' prowess in tracking down such missing shipments had been touted to Howard Herman at the country club. Childers always asked a new client what had prompted his selection, both testing his means of marketing his wares and taking elementary precautions. Herman had been embarrassingly grateful when the errant shipment was located in a warehouse in Peoria.

"Was it stolen?"

"I have no proof of that," Childers said. "It could merely have been a misshipment."

"A misshipment!"

"Mr. Herman, I have known cases of forty-car freight trains being mislaid."

"I'd like to sue that sonofabitch in Peoria."

"Don't. I persuaded him not to charge you for storage."

Herman got rosy red with anger. His disposition was not that of a man firmly in control of his fate. An investigation into Fox River Casing suggested why. Herman's father, Nathan, had been in fireworks until the early forties, when a successful bid for a government munitions contract had transformed a modest and seasonal business into a thriving concern that altered its name to Fox River Casing.

If fireworks depended on a single season, small-arms ammunition depended on war, or so Nathan Herman had thought. It is doubtful he would have altered the nature of his business if government money had not been lavishly available in those frightening years when the United States was turning itself into the arsenal of democracy. With the coming of peace, so Howard Herman had told Childers—part of his inquiry into Herman's company had been effected by becoming the confidant of the munitions maker—Nathan Herman hoped to sell out to one of the larger and more established munitions makers and turn to something more in harmony with his normally pacific nature. If the truth were known, Nathan Herman's conscience had bothered him when he produced nothing more lethal than fireworks. He could not bear to read post-Fourth of July newspaper accounts of blindings, burns, and losses of fingers or worse due to the careless handling of fireworks. In his heart he sympathized with the crusaders who wished to outlaw fireworks, despite the fact that the success of the campaign would have impoverished him.

But the war came and Fox River Fireworks became Fox River Casing, the noncommittal name a precaution against the espionage then much feared. The government underwrote the cost of new buildings and of the high wall topped by cyclone fencing that surrounded the plant. Nathan Herman had prospered, and if he was heartsore at the source of his success, he took comfort from the conviction that the war was just and Hitler must be defeated. He owed that defeat to his people and to his country, but after the war...

But the war never really ended. No sooner had Nathan begun negotiations to sell his firm than the Korean War made it inadvisable to sell. He was urged to continue to do his part, and he did, bringing his son Howard into the company.

Howard's father had been dead twelve years now and Fox River Casing was still a family concern. Lionel Childers ascertained that things had become rockier and rockier for Howard. There had been no favorable response to the overtures he made to the major munitions makers and without a buyer he could not liquidate a business that depended increasingly on minor conflicts around the globe and the whims of the United States Congress. Howard Herman became profanely eloquent on the subject of the Honorable Wilfrid Volkser. Vietnam had not been the respite to Fox River Casing Childers would have imagined it. The prudent Pentagon had sufficient small-arms ammunition in inventory for several such engagements and the resupply contracts did little more than keep the company afloat. Fox River Casing was tied to the fluctuating fortunes of foreign military aid, and Howard could not afford to be indifferent to the purchases made by the countries involved in the Mideast conflict.

"We cannot abandon Israel," Howard Herman said, but his bright eyes were elsewhere than on his listener. "We have moral obligations to guarantee her right to exist."

"Tell it to Volkser," Childers suggested gently.

"I have! The idiot has become a misguided moralizer."

"Aaron Leib will put an end to him."

"Yes."

Childers did not press the point. Herman could scarcely voice his feelings about Aaron Leib the way he freely castigated Representative Volkser, but Childers knew how Leib had taunted Howard Herman, had made the president of the reeling Fox River Casing suffer at his hands. Herman, Leib had said more than once, was willing to earn his bread selling arms to those whose avowed intention was to drive the Israelis into the sea. The cruelest thing about this accusation was that it was true. In the immemorial manner of armament manufacturers, Howard Herman sold his product indiscriminately, and though he tried to keep uninformed about the ultimate destination of his products, in his heart he knew Aaron Leib was justified in his accusation. Of course Leib could afford to be pure of heart. He had sold his own company for millions and had the financial underpinning to be unequivocal in his ethics. But if Aaron Leib objected to only some purchasers of the arms of American manufacturers, Wilfrid Volkser was determined that the country he loudly professed to love and serve should get out of the arms-supply business altogether.

"Meaning the business should be picked up by other countries. The idiot ought to know that arms will be gotten in one way or another."

"But not from us," Childers said, echoing the fruity tones of the congressman.

"The mood of the country is changing," Herman brooded.

"We're getting soft," Childers suggested.

Herman's face indicated that, like his father before him, he did not have his heart in the product he manufactured. But he had lost all room for maneuver. He was no longer able to think beyond the short term. His fate depended on the passage of the foreign aid appropriation Wilfrid Volkser was dedicated to defeating.

Lionel Childers, on the other hand, thought both short term and long. Herman found his a sympathetic ear when he wanted to expatiate on the need for the passage of the foreign aid bill. Reviewing these favorable facts, savoring his second chocolate sundae, Lionel Childers envisaged himself at the helm of the concern founded by Nathan Herman and managed with only mixed results by Howard.

"Go public," he urged Howard. "Put your stock on the market."

"Who would buy it?" Howard keened.

"There would be buyers," Lionel Childers assured him. "There would be buyers."

13

On the second day after the shooting of Aaron Leib, Chief Robertson called Phil Keegan in to tell him he had talked with both the FBI and the CIA and neither agency had anything new on the killing.

"Or they're not talking," he said significantly. "Perhaps their hands are tied by diplomatic considerations."

"Did they ask for any information?"

Robertson's smile was tolerant. He let Keegan go. What could the Fox River police possibly have that would be instructive to the FBI and CIA?

"Have you seen any strangers around the site?" Keegan asked Horvath.

"What do you mean?"

"Robertson thinks the FBI and CIA have

things well in hand, though they may be hampered by political considerations."

Horvath listened attentively, but his wide Slavic face did not betray any reaction to Keegan's irony.

Keegan said, "What have we found?"

Two slugs had been found, one that had passed through Aaron Leib and been ground down by the tire of the golf cart passing over it. Another had been found at the bottom of Howard Herman's golf bag.

"So someone really did take a shot at him too."

"Well, two shots were taken."

"From the same weapon?"

"We don't know yet."

"Get hold of the slug they dug out of the stands at Wrigley Field. That is, if political and diplomatic considerations will permit the Chicago police to release it."

Routine. Routine. Phil Keegan could sing its praises endlessly and point to case after case where it had been just dull unimaginative plodding that had removed whatever mystery hovered over such murders as came the way of the Fox River police. Another sort of soul than his might be stirred by the prospect of an exotic poison, a wholly unsuspected murderer, the twist within a twist that had everyone on the edge of his chair in the final scene when master sleuth Philip Keegan, outwardly unprepossessing, but ah, inwardly a maze of intuitions, logical leaps, and gifted with an infallible scent for guilt, revealed the identity of the villain.

It just didn't work that way. They had slugs, now they needed a weapon. Once they had a gun, the gun would have an owner, and then... And then. What prevented this killing from falling quickly into place was international politics, than which Phil Keegan could imagine no more irrational factor. He was equipped to deal with acts of violence between particular people, acts springing from personal motives, but if the slaying of Aaron Leib had been the deed of a faceless stranger representing an ideology at odds with Leib's, then the tried and true ways of establishing a relation between Leib and his killer were inapplicable. Routine would be a waste of time.

"Let the federal boys worry about it, Phil," Chief Robertson said some hours later, stopping by on his way out to an early lunch: an hour of racquet ball, a brisk shower, and then a low-cal repast with

Congressman Volkser. "Come along, Phil. What he wants is a report on the Leib case."

"There's nothing to report."

"From here anyway. Who knows what the others have turned up?"

"Maybe Volkser should lunch with the FBI," Keegan growled.

"I understand Franks and Threpplewaite will be there."

"I won't be able to make it."

"I'll let you know how they're coming with their investigation."

Seated at his desk, Keegan listened to Robertson's audible departure down the hall, the booming voice, the glad hand—you would think the chief was running for election right here in the department. But of course the source of patronage lay elsewhere, and Robertson's bonhomie was the reflex of a lifetime. Without his political friends he would be writing traffic citations. Maybe Robertson could accept the notion that a killing on the country club golf course in Fox River should be left to wiser heads, but Phil Keegan could not.

He phoned down for a car and, fuming, descended in the elevator to the garage. He had pulled out into traffic before he realized where he was going, but he would never have admitted this to anyone else. The reasons for talking again to Mrs. Aaron Leib were logical and compelling.

"Captain," she said, when Keegan was admitted to a sun porch that, on this morning, truly deserved its name. Tile floor, trellises alive with flowers, a light breeze in the pale yellow curtains, and Helen Leib in her rocker sipping coffee. Her manner was visibly less patient than before. "I have told your friends everything, Captain. I thought I had told you the same yesterday. This is beginning to seem like harassment."

"My friends?"

"A Mr. Franks and a Mr. Threpplewaite."

For an antic moment, Keegan wanted to deny he knew these men, or to suggest they were reporters posing as police investigators—anything to reclaim jurisdiction.

"Just routine, Mrs. Leib. Yesterday you suggested that you and your husband were not on the best of terms."

"I beg your pardon. I recall no such suggestion."

"You said in effect that your life together was based on not prying into what the other was doing."

"I meant that ours was a mature, trusting relationship, Captain. Nothing more."

"We've been talking to others, Mrs. Leib."

"I'm sure you have."

"Of course people can be malicious. I know that."

"What do you mean?"

"Frankly, I'm often surprised at the lurid interpretations that others, even friends, can put on a marriage. Even on a mature, trusting relationship such as yours."

Helen Leib sighed. "I will not ask you to repeat the gossip you've picked up."

"That saves us both a lot of time. I have no intention of bringing you slanderous stories. Was your husband faithful?"

One side of her mouth went up and her eyes crinkled, then opened as if in genuine wonderment. "Faithful," she repeated as she might have repeated "Stanley steamer," "Remember the Maine," "chastity."

"Then he wasn't?"

"If you are asking if he had other women, I'm sure he did. I would be surprised in the extreme if he had not. Captain, we are in the fourth quarter of the twentieth century."

It was an asset in his work that Keegan's

feelings seldom managed to alter the expression on his face. Would she, if he asked whether she had been faithful to Aaron Leib, respond in the same way? Phil Keegan did not want to think about it. Not unless it had some bearing on the death of her husband, he didn't. He persisted in thinking the women he came into contact with in the more sordid corners of police work were untypical, that the majority of women were as his wife had been, and his mother.

"Have you any idea who these women might be?"

"Are you asking me for names?"

"Could you give them?"

"Captain, even if I could, I wouldn't. I detect moral disapproval in your manner. That is your privilege, I suppose, but it is a personal privilege. If you let it guide you in looking into the causes of Aaron's death, you are simply going to waste your time and cause unnecessary embarrassment. Mr. Franks and Mr. Threpplewaite were quite certain that the motivation behind the killing was political. It is the only explanation that makes sense. My husband was a vital, vibrant human being, he had a lust for life. But he was always careful and considerate.

He would never have become emotionally involved if that could possibly have led to fireworks."

Fireworks. The word hung in the sunroom air as earlier the word "faithful" had. Keegan asked himself why he was pursuing this idiotic line of questioning. Aaron Leib had been a womanizer. Both he and Horvath had encountered this truth about the dead man in nearly every interview, but those who spoke of it did so much as Mrs. Leib did, with acceptance, without surprise; in the case of the men, even with grudging admiration. It mystified Phil Keegan that a man who had professed such a thirst for justice in the case of Israel could be indifferent to those parts of the Decalogue emphasized in his own moral training, specifically the sixth and ninth Commandments. He remembered an effort to rally youth to chastity under the banner of the Fighting 69th. That number, alas, had taken on an unsavory connotation and the organization would now be thought to be battling for perversion.

Fireworks. Fox River Casting. Howard Herman. Herman was one of the few who had not alluded to Leib's extramarital activity; but then, Herman had other grievances against Leib.

When Mrs. Leib reluctantly took him to the den in which Aaron Leib had done such work as he did at home, Keegan had the impression the room had already been emptied of significance.

"The others wanted to see this room too," she said.

"Did they take anything?"

"Not unless they did so without my permission. They would need my permission, I trust."

"Of course."

The room might have been an annex of the Israeli consulate. There were framed photographs of the Holy Land on the walls, apparently taken by Aaron Leib, at least some of them. In more than one he himself appeared, a confident bronze figure smiling into the camera, his arms about his companions.

"That man is the mayor of Jerusalem," Mrs. Leib said.

"How often did your husband go to Israel?"

"I stopped counting. Several times a year. There was a time when he talked of moving there, but he couldn't have done it. The danger unnerved him terribly. He had great admiration for those who lived there. That drove him, I think. A kind of guilt. He was determined to do as much for them as possible. Short of living with them."

"Did that disappoint you?"

"I have never been there. I'm not Jewish, you know."

"I didn't know."

Keegan looked at a photograph of Leib with two girls, an orange grove in the background.

"That's Aaron's kibbutz."

"How do you mean?"

"It's where we would have lived if ... It's in the north, near the Golan Heights." She pointed to a spot on a framed map of Israel. "Maximum danger. It fascinated Aaron, but I knew he wasn't that brave. Perhaps he wasn't brave at all."

Keegan regarded the photographed face of Aaron Leib. The expression seemed no less brave than those of the two girls with him. Brave or not, the danger had pursued Aaron Leib home and caught up with him on the fifteenth fairway of the golf course.

"Who are the girls?"

Mrs. Leib squinted at the picture, but it was a perfunctory inspection. She shrugged. "Just some girls."

He was glad to go. No matter how he revolved the Aaron Leib matter, its center of gravity remained the Middle East. On the way back downtown, he had half made up his mind to tell Horvath that they would waste no more time on it. Let the Franks and Threpplewaites handle it. It was not a local matter.

But when he got downtown, Cy Horvath had just received news of the automobile.

"A farmer called the sheriff about it. It was just sitting there on the road. He didn't like it."

"Whose car is it?"

"It belongs to a local woman."

"A woman!"

When the information came through from vehicle registration, Keegan and Horvath set out together to Gladys Lubins' address.

"Lubins," Horvath said, when they were coming up the ramp from the basement garage. Sunlight suddenly altered the lieutenant's face from shadow into light. "Funny. I stopped at Volkser's office."

"Did he have an alibi?" Keegan asked

dryly, then immediately regretted it. He reminded himself of Robertson. "What did you find?"

"Nothing. I talked with a guy named Chuck Howard, some kind of aide. The congressman was in the Rayburn Office Building in Washington when Leib was shot."

"What's funny about the name Lubins?"

"Nothing's funny about the name." Horvath had had ethnic sensitivity before it became a virtue. "It's just that that's the name of Volkser's administrative assistant."

"Not a common name."

"There's only one in the book."

That one, Gladys Lubins, did not answer her door. In the next yard, a middle-aged woman in shorts and halter was spraying rose bushes, her eyes on the two policemen. The white powdery cloud emerging from her sprayer was missing the roses.

"She's not home," she called.

Keegan crossed the lawn to her. "Have you seen Mrs. Lubins today?"

"She works."

"Where?"

"Are you police?"

"That's right." He showed his credentials

and had an annoying thought. "Any other police been here this morning?"

"Any other? How many kinds are there?"

"Where does Mrs. Lubins work?" Horvath had joined them, and the woman seemed to find the lieutenant's Slavic impassivity reassuring. She spoke to Cy.

"What kind of police are you?"

"How many kinds are there?" Cy said. "Does Mrs. Lubins have more than one car?"

"Is that a crime?" The woman's manner seemed saucy with Cy.

"She does drive, doesn't she?"

"So that's it, her driving. She told me she just put the tickets in her glove compartment and to hell with it." Sweat trickled down the woman's throat and lost itself in the damp cleavage of her halter.

"A Chevy Nova?" Cy asked.

"Don't ask me the names of cars. I lost track after the Edsel. Wasn't that a car?"

"There was a division of opinion," Keegan said, then wished he hadn't. Horvath could handle the woman, he could not. She told Cy her name was Amy Janov, punctuating it with a little burst from her rose sprayer.

"Central High?"

The damp face became attractive with a smile. "You too? What's your name?"

"Horvath. Cy Horvath."

"My God!" She stepped back, as if to get perspective. "You look like you could suit up right now and still play football."

"What was your name?"

"Rullo. Amy Rullo. Don't ask me what class."

"Probably way after mine," Horvath said with a gallantry that surprised Keegan. "You know Mrs. Lubins well?"

A shake of the head. "A libber. Mrs. Independence. Or Miz Independence. She can't make as much money as she claims, but she's doing pretty good."

"Is that her husband who works for Volkser?"

"She hasn't got any husband. Divorced. Who's Volkser?"

Cy got back to cars. The woman had only one car and she worked at Fox River Realty. Amy Rullo Janov offered to go inside and look up the number, but they thanked her and went back to the car. Cy had taken off his jacket and carried it thrown over his shoulder. At the car he turned and waved good-by. Amy waved back, with the hand holding the sprayer, and a small cloud formed above her, then dispersed. Keegan had the impression Horvath was sucking in his stomach and striking an athlete's pose.

When Cy got behind the wheel, Keegan called in for the address of Fox River Realty. As they headed for it, Horvath said, "Lubins must be the guy she divorced."

"Well, her name is Mrs. Lubins."

"There's no other Lubins in the book."

"The Fox River or the Greater Chicago?" Keegan asked.

"The Fox River."

"He probably lives in Washington. Congressmen keep an address in their district, but I doubt that their assistants could afford it. What's he like?"

"Lubins? I didn't get to see him. The place was pretty busy, all kinds of people wanting to see Volkser."

"Was he there?"

"Holding court." Cy clamped his mouth shut on this rare metaphor. "I talked to this guy Howard."

"What did you ask him?"

But it would have been impossible for Horvath to reconstruct the way in which he managed to get people to talk to him, even people who moved in the sort of circles Chuck Howard must. If Keegan knew Cy Horvath, the lieutenant would have had the congressman's aide considering it a civic duty to instruct a dumb cop on the basics of political life while Cy no doubt stood there nodding and grinning like a slow learner. Cy had been given a sketch of the flash decision to return to the district when they learned of Leib's death, the crush of the press at O'Hare, Volkser's grief and indignation at the shooting.

"That was bull, but Howard himself seemed genuinely sorry."

"Why?"

Horvath shrugged. "He said he'd never met Leib."

"And Lubins wasn't there?"

Horvath shook his head, his brows lifting. He fished a notebook from his shirt pocket and, driving with one hand, began to flip through its pages.

"I'll look it up for you," Keegan said nervously.

"You couldn't read my writing."

"And you can't drive and read at the same time. What the hell are you looking for?"

Cy pulled over to the curb, flipped back several pages, stopped, and the frown went away. "It's Gladys all right, but not Lubins."

"Tell me about it," Keegan said patiently.

"One of the women Leib was mixed up with. Gladys Horkin." Cy put away the notebook and pulled into traffic again. "What did Mrs. Leib say?"

"She knew and she didn't care."

"Come on."

"They had a mature, trusting relationship."

Neither of them spoke the rest of the way to Fox River Realty. Horvath might ripple a muscle out of nostalgia for the benefit of Amy Rullo Janov, but he would no more think infidelity quaint than Keegan did. Keegan had the fleeting thought that the two of them represented a discarded morality, and that attempts to enforce it in a community that no longer believed in it were ridiculous. Did Roger Dowling ever feel this way? Maybe. But in the Church there were precedents for everything: the Holy Roman Empire, but the catacombs too. Most of the world was now in a catacomb condition as far as religion went. Not in the U.S.A., of course. Here it was only quaint.

Had religion ever had to face up to amused indifference before? Keegan pushed the thought away. However much people might jump in and out of the wrong beds, the consensus against murder was still there, and it was a murder they were investigating, not the decayed sexual morals of selected citizens.

The receptionist gave them a receptive smile until Keegan told her who they were. The eyes widened and she pressed her hands flat on the desk.

"Is Mrs. Lubins in?"

"She uses the name Gladys Horkin professionally."

Keegan heard Horvath inhale through his nose. Before the girl could lift the interoffice phone, Keegan laid his hand on hers.

"Which office is hers?"

The girl nodded toward a closed door behind which music played very loudly. Horvath was at the door in three strides but, John to Keegan's St. Peter, he waited for his boss to knock once and push the door open.

Behind her desk, the woman was in the process of lighting a cigarette. She released the lighter, extinguishing its flame, and studied the two men through exhaled smoke.

"Come in," she said ironically. "Isn't Rosemary out there?"

"Mrs. Lubins?"

"Who are you?"

"My name is Captain Keegan. This is Lieutenant Horvath."

"Captain? Lieutenant? All right, where is it?"

"Do you mind if I sit?"

"Be my guest. What is it, a subpoena? You got me. I can't escape." She held out her hand.

"I don't have a subpoena," Keegan said.

"We want to ask you a few questions." Horvath now stood by the window, where an air conditioner competed with the racket from the radio on the woman's desk. Her eyes dropped to it when Keegan glared. She turned down the volume. "Sorry. It helps me think."

"Are you expecting a subpoena, Mrs. Lubins?"

"When someone calls me Mrs. Lubins I expect anything."

"I understand you're divorced."

"He threatened to apply for alimony. Just a bad joke, I thought. A crack at me for proving I was good for something other than cooking and cleaning house and...And the rest of it."

"We're investigating the killing of Aaron Leib," Horvath said.

"What kind of car do you drive, Mrs. Lubins?"

"Stop calling me that. My name is Gladys Horkin. What about my car?"

"Do you drive a car?"

"Of course I drive a car. I sell real estate. Why are you asking about my car if you're investigating..."

"The shooting of Aaron Leib," Horvath repeated with quiet insistence. "You knew Mr. Leib, didn't you?"

Gladys Horkin put her cigarette to her lips and inhaled deeply. She might have been deliberately defying the surgeon general, decades of statistics, her own better judgment. She was certainly defying her visitors.

"I don't like this," she said. "I don't like it one damned bit. What right do you have to come bursting in on me and asking all these questions?"

Keegan said, "A Chevrolet Nova registered in your name was found abandoned this morning on Raspberry Road. That's County Road DD. It had been there for two days."

"About a mile from the Fox River Country Club," Horvath added.

"Aaron Leib was shot while golfing at the Fox River Country Club."

"A number of people have mentioned your name in connection with Aaron Leib." Horvath had moved away from the air conditioner for this antiphonal narrative.

"Those are merely facts, of course," Keegan said. "Would you care to comment on them?"

Gladys's mouth had fallen open. "Do you mean you're connecting me with the death of Aaron Leib?"

"Is that your only comment on the facts that brought us here?"

"You do own a Chevy Nova, License number..." Horvath opened his notebook but she answered with a shout.

"No! No, I don't. I sold that car."

Keegan looked at Horvath. Cy shook his head. "The car is registered in your name. When did you sell it?"

She made an impatient motion with her hand. "Months ago."

"To whom?"

The woman got up and started around the desk. Horvath moved as if to intercept her,

143

and she looked at him with disgust. She jabbed at the door with her finger.

"Close it." Her lips formed the words but she did not speak them.

Horvath closed the door.

"I sold it to Rosemary. I signed the title and..."

"Rosemary is the receptionist?"

Horvath was back at the door. He opened it and left the room. Gladys sat forward, her lower lip drawn between her teeth, listening.

"She's not here," Horvath called.

Of course she wasn't there, not if Gladys whatever-her-name-was was telling the truth. Their conversation would have been audible in the outer office.

"Rosemary who?" Keegan was on his feet now. He felt like a jackass. It was not the kind of mistake you can guard against, but it didn't hurt any less when you made it. There had been something in the receptionist's manner that should have warned him. Bah. Hindsight. She had been only a girl surprised to be confronted by two policemen.

"Walsh." Gladys's voice was a whisper. Too bad she hadn't spoken that way earlier.

"Where does she live?"

"Look." Gladys came around the desk

144

and they joined Horvath in the outer office. She put her hand on Keegan's arm. "Captain, that car was stolen."

"Stolen." Keegan looked at her sadly.

"I mean it. It was parked out back and when Rosemary was going to leave it wasn't there."

"When was that?"

She hesitated, then said, "Day before yesterday."

"The car was abandoned day before yesterday too."

"Who says so?"

"A farmer."

Horvath said, "Aaron Leib and the car of your secretary—you say you sold it to her—found abandoned near the spot from which was shot..."

The woman lifted her hand to her mouth, palm outward, as if to ward off bad news.

"Rosemary Walsh first missed her car two days ago?"

"That's what she...Yes. You can see the parking area out back from my office. She looked out that window and saw it was missing."

"Did she report it?"

"I don't know."

"Weren't you here at the time?"

"Yes, I was here at the time. And Rosemary was here at the time. Her car wasn't. We were here till after seven."

"Why did she run off?"

"What do you mean, run off?" Gladys looked at her watch. "It's her lunch time."

"Where does she eat lunch?"

"Search me."

Horvath said, "Tell us about Aaron Leib."

"Tell you about Aaron Leib?" She sat on a desk top as if needing support before this display of stupidity.

"What was your relationship with him?"

"Realtor to client. I was in on the purchase of his house."

"Just a business relationship?"

"We were friendly. It's the way I do business. This is a people-meeting job, you know, and I love people. Most of my clients end by becoming friends of mine."

"Then Leib's death must have hit you pretty hard."

"It didn't surprise me."

"Why not?"

"After that shot in Cub Park? I figured it was only a matter of time."

146

"Sad," Horvath said, but this did not prompt any emotional outpouring from Gladys. Apparently, if all her clients became her friends, the concept had to be diluted. Back in her office, they satisfied themselves that, with the radio and air conditioner going, a fleet of automobiles could be moved from the back parking lot without being heard by Gladys Horkin Lubins.

"I feel to blame for it," Gladys said.

"How do you mean?"

"I always keep a spare ignition key under the floor mat of my car. I did that with the Nova. Rosemary picked up the habit from me."

"A car thief doesn't need a key," Horvath said.

Keegan left Horvath there, to wait for Rosemary Walsh; he himself took a cab to St. Hilary's where he was in time for Roger Dowling's noon Mass. The old church was dark and cool and there were perhaps a dozen worshipers as Father Dowling moved with reverent swiftness through the liturgy. There were days, and this was one of them, when Phil Keegan found it irresistible to daydream of the life that would have been his if he had not, years and years before, left the seminary, joined the army, entered the military police, and then joined the force. He imagined himself standing at that altar, offering the bread and wine, praying for the people and himself. It seemed so impossibly peaceful and untrammeled a life that Phil Keegan rubbed his face with his hands to erase the thought. He was forty-nine years old. He was a widower, his children married. More important, he was captain of detectives in the Fox River police force. If God had meant him to be a priest, he would have helped him do better in Latin years ago. It was strange to think that an inability to learn Latin was no longer an impediment to becoming a priest.

"Come have lunch," Roger Dowling said when Phil went into the sacristy after Mass.

"Are you sure?"

"Of course I'm sure." Roger Dowling seemed amused by the thought that it was Mrs. Murkin and not himself who ran the rectory.

Omelets, cucumber and tomato salad, iced tea. Sometimes Mrs. Murkin's simplest meals were the best. Keegan told Roger Dowling how he had been wasting his time since the killing of Aaron Leib.

"The man's wife knew he was running around and it didn't bother her in the least. Can you believe that?"

"No."

"Roger, it's a very different world out there. Half the time I don't believe it myself, but it is different. What's that term? Post-Christian. That's what it is."

"Where was Mrs. Leib when her husband was killed?"

"Under a dryer in a beauty shop in the lobby of the Fox River Hotel. Mr. Conrad, who is as pretty as his clients, will attest that..."

"Then you did consider her?"

"Routine."

The nice thing about Roger Dowling was that he was as interested in the details of police routine as he was in the surprises that came along. The abandoned car fascinated him, and he could not hear enough of the visit to Fox River Realty, the exchange with Gladys Horkin Lubins, the skipping of Rosemary Walsh.

"Then you don't believe she went to lunch as Mrs. Horkin said?"

"Mrs. Lubins. Or Miz Horkin. Cy stayed

there to make sure."

"Of course if the car was stolen..."

"If?"

14

Running was wrong. It was crazy.

Rosemary realized this even as she slipped out of the office, raced to the corner, and boarded a bus halted there by a red light. She banged on the closed door and the driver looked down testily but then opened the door with a smile. He even forgave her for not having the correct change.

"Just give what you can afford," he said breezily.

"I only have a dollar."

He waved it away. "This isn't a regular stop anyway."

For that matter, the bus was all but empty. The light changed, the bus lurched forward, and she moved involuntarily down the aisle. A couple—they couldn't have been more than teen-agers—were locked amorously in the back seat. The girl glared malevolently at Rosemary. An elderly woman sat opposite the exit in the middle of the vehicle speaking to herself, aloud and vehemently. No wonder the driver had welcomed another passenger.

It was after she sat down that she told herself it had been crazy to run away like this. Now, as the distance from the office grew, she could imagine herself being as sassy with the police as Gladys was. After all, her car had been stolen. What did it matter that she had not yet gone down to register the title in her own name, or that she had not reported the theft? For all she knew, they had found the car.... No, she decided, stopping these thoughts. No. She had been right to go.

Go. Where was she going? The thought grew in her that her Fox River idyll was over. It had been over ever since the missed assassination attempt in Cub Park. How foolish she had been to believe she could so easily escape from her past.

If only her car had not been taken. An hour ago, when she told Gladys about her missing car, the older woman stared open-mouthed at Rosemary.

"Well, that settles that."

"What do you mean?"

"I had hoped you'd taken it."

"And kept it for two days?" But Gladys's laugh sailed up the scale. She sat forward. "I suppose that extra key was still under the doormat."

Rosemary nodded, abject. She wanted to believe that it was only a theft, some kids nosing around, finding the key, deciding to take a joy ride. Kids like that couple in the back of the bus. Necking or worse. Ye gods.

Of course she didn't spend the day checking to see if her car was still out back. It had been there at noon, she was sure of that. She had noticed it when she came back from lunch. Had it been there when she took the cab to Sharon's? She had assumed it was, but she did not really know. If it wasn't there then, it would have been stolen sometime during the afternoon when she had been alone in the office. Gladys had not come back to the office after going on her lunch hour. She told Gladys the car had not been there when she left the night before.

"I came into your office and looked out the window."

"Why?"

"I don't know. I just did. Maybe I always do that before leaving—look out, see the car. I'm still not used to the fact that I own it. Owned it."

"You'll get it back, Rosemary. Don't worry. Did you take out insurance?"

Gladys had insisted she do this but Rosemary had not called an insurance agent. She hadn't registered the title either. Nor did she want to notify the police when the car was missing.

"I'll do it," Gladys had said. "Don't worry."

For a mad moment, when those two detectives stood before her desk, she had thought they were there about her car, that Gladys had reported it and they had hurried right out.

The bus began to fill as it neared downtown and when Rosemary got out she had to push her way to the door. She found a cab stand but no taxis. Where was she going? St. Hilary's. The sense of well-being and safety that had attended her sleep in Mrs. Murkin's bed was difficult to understand when she thought of what had driven her to that refuge, but the rectory had been a sanctuary, a place where no harm could come to her. Not even Mrs. Murkin's story of how her husband had been killed in that bedroom robbed Rosemary of her conviction that in St. Hilary's parish house she was safe. The same feeling had accompanied her to work and had not really been dispelled until she listened to the odd exchange taking place in Gladys's office.

Gladys and Aaron Leib. Leib had to be the man of whom Gladys spoke both guardedly and with embarrassing frankness, as if she had made a conquest rather than suffered a defeat. Perhaps it had been both, though Rosemary found Gladys unconvincing in the role of the sensuous career girl who took her pleasure where she found it while avoiding ties that bind. After all, Gladys had expected her lover to get a divorce and marry her.

"It got me out of my marriage, if nothing else. And there was plenty else."

"Does he live here in Fox River?"

"My husband?"

"No. The man."

Gladys had looked mysterious, actually twisting her lips with her fingers and throwing away the key. It was like crossing your heart and hoping to die, a gesture completely out of harmony with Gladys's tough-gal manner. When Rosemary heard those detectives mention Aaron Leib, it seemed she had always known the identity of Gladys's mysterious Jewish lover. Aaron Leib, the man who had been shot! She was relieved that Gladys had not brought up the subject in the office; it was hardly something they could have chatted about as if it were just another item in the news. Yet how could Gladys have kept quiet about it?

After she got off the bus, Rosemary walked to St. Hilary's, well over a mile, but she could not stand on the street waiting for a cab and she had no idea what bus would take her to Father Dowling. Besides, by walking she kept her distance from her own apartment.

Mrs. Murkin did not seem surprised when Rosemary knocked on the kitchen door.

"I'm making omelets. How do you like yours?"

"Is Father Dowling in?"

"Just came back from Mass. He has a guest for lunch."

"Oh."

Mrs. Murkin looked at her. "I'll tell him you're here."

"No. No, I'll wait. Can I wait here?"

"Captain Keegan isn't company, Rosemary. I'll just tell Father you're here and he'll want you to join them."

The housekeeper sailed off into the dining room and Rosemary quickly let herself outside and crossed the lawn to the side door of the church. Inside there was the lingering smell of candles and an old man standing in the main aisle. As she went swiftly along a side aisle he advanced toward the front of the church, then stopped again. He did an imitation of a genuflection. Saying the Stations. It was like coming upon someone using an abacus. Rosemary left the church by the main door and hurried to the corner, cut across the playground of the school, and began to move faster. Not knowing where she was going seemed to quicken her pace. Where on earth could she go?

And then, as she had two days before, she knew.

Sharon's.

The Hermans.

Maybe Billy would be there.

15

With Denny Lubins once more in control, Chuck Howard's job was considerably easier than it had been since the moment Volkser first felt the overwhelming urge to return to the district because of the news of Aaron Leib's death. Nor was Maggie Powers, who ran the district office, overburdened once the congressman and Lubins went off to lunch with Chief Robertson.

"You come along, Denny," Volkser had said importantly. "I want liaison established with the investigation. I want to be kept apprised of every development."

"Robertson doesn't know his ass from his elbow."

Volkser thought about that. "Well, there is a resemblance. Last night I spoke with two men, Franks and Threpplewaite. They are conducting a real investigation. They'll be lunching with us, but I want Robertson to give this thing a local dimension."

"Did you reach Fletcher, Charles?" Volkser asked Chuck Howard. He insisted on calling him Charles, as if he were a butler or valet. But if Volkser had a valet, his name was Dennis Lubins.

"On behalf of the Republican Party, he thanks you for your expression of sympathy."

"Is that all?"

"I'll talk to him, Wilf," Lubins said.

"Do that."

"Leib wasn't even their candidate," Howard complained to Lubins when the congressman disappeared into the inner office with Maggie in tow.

"He would have been, everyone knew that."

"Lucky Wilf."

"What do you mean?" Denny asked.

"How many incumbents have their opposition removed by Arabs?"

"Yeah."

"Did you see Gladys?"

The question stopped Lubins on his way into Volkser's office. He turned slowly, a pained expression on his face. "Gladys who?"

Chuck Howard shrugged. "Don't ask me. I don't know any ex-wives named Gladys."

"Why would I have seen her?"

"Why would you come to Fox River for a week right smack dab in the middle of committee hearings?"

"Three days," Lubins corrected. "For the Cubs' home stand. That's what I came for."

"Masochist."

"Yeah."

Magikist. Billboards all over Chicago. Cleaners, something or other. Giant plush red lips puckered over the traffic. They seemed to address their appeal to all poor benighted Cub fans.

"Were you there when..."

"They shot at the consul? I was there. Not that I knew it at the time."

"Who won the game?"

"You're kidding."

Maggie came out when Lubins went in and she stopped to smile at Chuck. "You look sort of dumb."

"It's part of my job description. Let's go have a beer."

"At eleven in the morning?"

"I know it's late but I had a hard night."

"Don't tell me about it."

They went to Shannons, where there was sawdust on the floor and bowls of peanuts in the booths and a slatternly waitress who tried to interest them in hamburgers as complements to the beer.

"Avoid the luncheon rush," she urged.

They decided to avoid the hamburgers instead. Maggie, still on the sunny side of thirty, began as usual to speak of her dream of being shifted to the Washington staff.

"You wouldn't like it," Chuck assured her. "Do you know what the ratio of women to men in the District is?"

"I'll bet you do."

"Washington is not the real world. Maggie, I envy you." He hunched over the table. "Maybe I'll ask to be transferred here. You and I could tell lies about Volkser together."

"You'd actually want to work in Fox River?"

"I love Fox River. Fox River is my native town."

"Mine too."

"There you are. I love getting back here. We all do. Look at Denny Lubins."

"I'm not following you."

"He's been back for days."

"No." She shook her head.

"Yup. He came to watch the Cubs play."

"What did he do, turn right around and come back last night?"

"Now I'm not following you."

"He phoned me from Washington to check on arrangements."

"Oh, that. Last night?"

"Sure."

"That was after I talked to you?"

"What is this? Do you check up on each other?"

"I'm a spy for his wife."

"Isn't he divorced?"

"His wife doesn't believe in divorce."

Maggie cracked a peanut. "I know her, Chuck."

"I don't. I mean, I met her, but I never really got to know her."

"Quite a gal."

"She tells that to all the girls."

"No. She's making it big. Money and everything."

"And everything?"

Maggie nodded but looked away and Chuck was charmed by her confusion, almost virginal. But what exactly did Maggie know? He importuned the slattern for two more beers, again resisted her siren song on behalf of hamburgers, lit a cigarette.

"What do you know about Fletcher, Maggie?"

"Nothing. I'm no traitor."

"He's only a Republican. Some of them pay taxes, fight for the fatherland, even vote. As far as I can see, he's already conceded the next election."

"Well, after all, Wilfrid Volkser."

"Please, Maggie. Not between us. We know better. Fletcher's got a whole year to dig up somebody."

"That's what he'd have to do. Aaron Leib, to be exact. He was their only chance."

"Lucky us."

"That's not true, you know." It was her turn to lean across the table, an operation with interesting consequences for the downcast eye. "Leib was highly respected—here, in Chicago, all over the country. This could upset Wilfrid Volkser's apple cart, but good. On military aid. Better Aaron Leib as a living potential opponent than as a martyr on the other side."

"Shrewd. You ought to work in Washington."

"Put in a word for me, Chuck."

"I will, Maggie. I mean it."

He wondered if she were shrewd enough to put together the pieces of the conversation: Lubins, his ex-wife, Leib. She seemed to know a bit about Gladys Lubins, née Horkin. Would she know of the affair with Leib that had smashed up the marriage? And Dennis Lubins, whatever the ratio of women to men in Washington, was not reconciled to the loss of his wife. It was easy, on a couple of beers too early in the day, to imagine things. A vengeful Lubins returns to Fox River, stalking the man who had alienated his wife's affections and whose Zionism had led Lubins to push Wilfrid Volkser in the direction the congressman had gone, a pawn of Lubins' hatred of Aaron Leib. In the ball park, he tries and misses....

"Naw."

"Naw what?"

"A hamburger? Sorry. I don't have time. I've got things to do."

"Pardon me all to hell. This was your idea."

"Maggie, if you had any idea how you address my concupiscence."

"'Dear Sir?'"

"I like you. Come on, let's go."

He dropped her at the office and, from a public phone in the lobby, called Washington. The Southern drawl at the other end of the line was not, Chuck Howard suddenly realized, appropriate for the office of Wilfrid Volkser of Illinois.

"This is Chuck, honey. A small credit-card problem. Where was Mr. Lubins booked over the past three days?"

"You mean, where was he staying?"

"That's right. Where did he say we could get in touch with him?"

"Give me a minute. Do you want me to call you back?"

"No, I'll hold."

He had hoped that would get her Confederate rear in high gear, but he had five long minutes to watch the crowd skate across the granite floor of the huge lobby before she came back on the line. He tried to decipher the purposes of passersby from the expressions on their faces. No luck. But then who, looking at him with a phone to his ear, would guess he was trying to rid himself of the ridiculous thought that the administrative assistant of Congressman Wilfrid Volkser had shot and killed Aaron Leib?

"I don't find any note or anything, Mr. Howard."

"Thanks, Darleen. Miss me?"

"Mr. Howard, you know I do."

16

The thing went so smoothly Lennie could hardly believe it, but Childers proved himself to be a businessman in every way. No stupid questions, no need to mention the basis of the transaction, just a silent passing over of the envelope.

"Open it and count it."

"I trust you."

Childers shrugged and for a moment Lennie regretted not having opened the envelope. Was it large enough to contain ten thousand dollars? But he was the captive now of his own pride; he had said he trusted Childers and now he had to trust himself.

"A word of advice, Lennie."

Lennie stood before Childers' desk, a pupil called in to see the principal, waiting.

"Don't throw the money around. Go on living as you have been. Be smart."

Good advice. It was not what Lionel would have called disinterested advice, of course. He had a vested interest in Lennie's being smart. Their fates were linked now, no matter how removed from the facts Childers might feel, sitting there in his plush office high above Fox River. It was an odd thought, but Lionel Childers was in his power.

It was also an uncomfortable thought, since it cut both ways. Being smart seemed to dictate spending the night somewhere else than in his own apartment. Chicago? The thought of a quiet celebration, checking into a good hotel, appealed. But then, going down in the elevator, Lennie had the smartest thought of all. He would drop in on O'Boyle.

The parole officer sat scratching himself and chewing on a cigar behind his messy desk. He waved Lennie to a chair.

"Been keeping your nose clean, Lennie?"

"No, I been robbing banks."

"Nobody robs banks any more."

"Only bankers."

"You have a point."

Lennie knew he had a point. He settled back and began to tell O'Boyle about Ratchet, the computer whiz, who claimed he could rob the Chase Manhattan while seated at a console in Denver. Nothing to it. Foolproof.

"Then what was he doing in prison?"

"A fluke, O'Boyle."

They talked about flukes and O'Boyle warmed to the theme. The parole officer was more of an anarchist than most cons. He did not think nemesis or justice hunted down the wrongdoer. "Life is a lottery, Lennie. There's only a banana peel between respectability and farce. Ask any cop. If he's honest he'll admit that crooks are caught by pure chance."

"I'm keeping away from cops."

"Good. Good. How do you like working for Childers?"

"It's interesting." Lennie looked at his watch. "Say, how about having dinner with me?"

O'Boyle was torn between what he conceived to be the duties of his vocation and the tug of his wife and the three little O'Boyles. He came up with a compromise, picking up the phone. Lennie listened while

O'Boyle informed his wife they were having company for dinner. He seemed to be meeting resistance. Lennie held up his hand and shook his head but O'Boyle ignored him.

"About an hour," he told the phone, and hung it up. "I hope you like meat loaf."

"If you like Beefeater. I'll buy you a drink."

O'Boyle liked Irish whisky. Lennie ordered Scotch. It was like taking medicine. Lionel drank Scotch. Afterward they drove to O'Boyle's in O'Boyle's car. Perfect. Lennie wanted to laugh out loud. Talk about being smart. Not even Lionel Childers would have thought of anything as perfect as this, a night with his parole officer. It wasn't exactly an orgy in a Chicago hotel, not with the racket O'Boyle's kids made and the fact that Susan O'Boyle was clearly not in the mood to entertain one of her husband's ex-convicts. The meat loaf was too spicy and the baked potatoes were underdone, but Lennie had seldom enjoyed a meal more. Mrs. O'Boyle and the kids went to bed early, before ten, looking as if they had worn one another out, and Lennie and O'Boyle smoked cigars and, after the ten-o'clock news, discussed the horrible shooting on the fifteenth fairway of the Fox River Country Club.

"Where were we when that happened?" O'Boyle wondered. "In that bar?"

"No, it was earlier. When we were in your office."

O'Boyle accepted that. Lennie freshened his drink. The Scotch wasn't tasting any better. O'Boyle began to grumble about golf courses like the country club. He didn't seem all that high on Aaron Leib either.

"Never heard of the guy," Lennie said.

The advantage of drinking Scotch was that he had no desire at all to keep up with O'Boyle, who was lapping up the Jamesons as if tomorrow was a weekend. Now, there was a thought for you. How often was one's fate decided by hungover judges and lawyers and parole officers who can no longer focus their eyes? O'Boyle put his head back, closed his eyes, and fell asleep almost immediately, a glass containing little more than melted ice cubes in one hand, the neck of the Jamesons bottle in the other.

Lennie told himself he would wait until O'Boyle dropped the bottle, then leave.

It seemed better to wait lying on his side,

on the couch. He closed his eyes and when he opened them again birds were raising hell outside, the room was bright with dawn, and one of the little O'Boyles was sitting on the floor eating a bowl of corn flakes.

Lennie got the hell out.

Rita opened the door when she decided that whoever was on the bell was not going to go away.

"Geez, Lennie, give a girl a break. I haven't had three hours sleep."

"Who said anything about getting up?"

Whereupon he opened his paper sack to reveal two bottles of Chivas Regal. Rita, puffy faced, looking her age, wrapped in a pink robe with a sort of feathery edging, real class, stepped back and let him in. A couple of belts of Scotch and she looked a lot better. The life she led, she was lucky she didn't look worse.

"And what have you done to earn Lionel's esteem?" Rita asked. She seemed to be mimicking his own mimicry.

"You see much of him any more?" Lennie felt for and found the envelope in an inside pocket of his jacket, disguising the move by scratching himself à la O'Boyle. He didn't like a conversation where he couldn't remember what he had just said.

"How'm I going to see him without your knowing about it?"

"I don't want him to know about me seeing you."

"Are you crazy?"

"Just on weekdays."

"Lennie, he finds out about you, I lose a client."

"A client?"

"As Lionel would say."

They drank to her wit, but he wanted to get off the subject of Lionel. The less Rita knew the better, for him, for her. He offered to scramble some eggs, which he did, making a mess of it, and by the time he stumbled back to Rita with the results, she was so deeply asleep he couldn't wake her up. Poor kid, up all night, she needed her sleep. He sat on the edge of the bed and spooned scrambled eggs into his mouth, looking at Rita, thinking of what he knew and she did not. Out like a light, she looked almost innocent in the disheveled bed. Well, she was innocent. She had never killed anyone. That was funny, thinking never having killed someone was an accomplishment. He put the plate on the floor, got in beside Rita, and had no difficulty falling asleep.

He woke once and reached for her and when he couldn't find her called her name. For answer he got the sound of the toilet flushing. Reassured, he rolled over and once again let himself sink beneath the surface of a sea of Scotch.

The next time he woke up he was again alone in the bed. The shades were pulled and glowed dully with early evening light. There was no answer when he called Rita's name. For five minutes he lay on his back, hands behind his head, trying to fight through the sluggishness. His skin felt dry and sensitive; he must have drunk two quarts of Scotch himself. He threw his legs over the side of the bed, found the floor, rose and stumbled across the room, arresting himself by getting a hand on the door frame. Wow.

"Rita?"

The place wasn't exactly silent because he could hear music from the apartment below, the one above, and those on either side. In the kitchen, the pan in which he had scrambled eggs looked accusingly at him, and he felt a dangerous rolling in his stomach. He made it to the bathroom in time. A much tidier room. There should be more evidence of Rita there. Standing at the sink, looking at himself in the medicine-cabinet mirror, he watched the thought form on his face. He eased open the door of the cabinet and looked at the all but empty shelves.

He careened back to the bedroom, plunged his hand inside his jacket. The envelope was gone. Jesus H. Christ. He stumbled back into the kitchen, looked into the tiny living room. It all looked the same, but then, it must come furnished. The closet. When he opened the door, he set off a tinkling of coat hangers. Cleaned out. She was gone.

He went into the kitchen and made coffee and drank it sitting at the kitchen table, looking out the window at a section of Chicago that seemed to be waiting for another fire. The situation was so classical it was funny, but not so funny that he felt like laughing. What he felt like doing was going back to bed and sleeping until his mind was clear. Then he would find Rita and his ten thousand dollars. He would find her if it took the rest of his life. And God help her when he got his hands on her.

The ringing of the phone lifted him from the chair and he actually looked around as if he had to hide from this electronic intruder. It kept on ringing until, in the mad hope she had changed her mind and was calling to beg his forgiveness, he picked up the phone.

He put it to his ear, saying nothing. The line was live but no one spoke on the other end. The breathing Lennie heard was his own. He moved the mouthpiece away from his mouth, keeping the receiver pressed to his ear. Was it a client?

"Rita?"

Lennie depressed the hook with two fingers, then put the phone back. The voice had been that of Lionel Childers. Too bad. For what he wanted he would have to call some other hustler. Lionel was going to miss Rita.

And then he knew he had to get the hell out of there. Childers' voice was a reminder that he had to get back to playing it smart. Smart. The thought of the missing money was enough to make a grown man cry.

17

Edna Hospers ran the St. Hilary Recreation Center with an efficiency that was not unwelcome to the elderly people who frequented the erstwhile parish school to participate in the bridge tournaments, the shuffleboard, the chess and pinochle, or simply to take advantage of the place as somewhere to bring one's knitting and have someone to talk to. Edna had started small and had not needed much encouragement from Father Dowling to expand. What had begun as a two-day-a-week enterprise now hummed along from Monday through Saturday and more often than not on Sundays as well. The baby-sitting service Edna called the St. Hilary Day Care Center was a godsend during the Sunday Masses, of course, and it seemed a natural extension of that to have coffee and doughnuts for those parishioners who chose to drift over after Mass, whether or not they had a child to retrieve. Edna's own kids spent the day with her, charter members of her day care center. Whenever more trendy pastors asked Father Dowling about his parish team, he was particularly glad to have Edna Hospers to talk about.

"What about adult education?" Monsignor Rath had asked.

"Our parish center is an education in itself."

Rath's smile was that of a man who refused to have his leg pulled. "I've had very good results with my Scripture seminar."

"Tell me about it."

Rath did so with pleasure. He seemed intent on turning his parishioners into Biblical scholars, and his talk was laced with reference to myths, the Middle Eastern mind, and other faintly debunking concepts. "We try to avoid any idolatry of the Word," Rath explained.

Father Dowling's experience with such study groups and seminars was small. The several he had attended as an observer, before he himself was assigned to parish work, seemed redolent of the worst aspects of the classroom. He who spoke was heard with sufferance, the listeners earning the right to speak themselves. Father Dowling wasn't sure he wanted to see lay people become amateur Biblical scholars. Jesus seemed able to get through to the receptive soul without footnotes.

Fortunately the parishioners of St. Hilary's showed little interest in the innovations that had revolutionized parish life in Chicago and, indeed, throughout the nation. Rath had spoken in hushed scandalized tones of Eastern parishes that continued to hold the traditional bazaars, huge affairs strung along several city blocks and running for days.

"It's a species of hustling," Rath growled.

Father Dowling decided not to go into too much detail about the St. Hilary Recreation Center with this otherworldly monsignor, a laborer certainly worthy of his hire without benefit of bazaars. Not that Edna ran a money-losing enterprise. She made a neat profit on coffee and doughnuts and on her baby-sitting service, but that profit simply covered the salary the parish paid her, a salary which, given the desertion of her husband Gene, she needed.

"Your friend Woodie is here today," Edna said to Father Dowling.

"Good. I told him of all the things there were to do here."

"He wants to talk to you."

Woodie stood on the sidelines watching two couples play shuffleboard and he seemed to be trying to grasp the point of the game.

"Hello, Mr. Wilson."

"Good morning, Reverend. Quite a place."

"Now that you've found it, I hope you'll come often. Mrs. Hospers will introduce you around."

Mr. Wilson held up a hand. "I nixed that. It's not my style. I like to make my own friends."

"That's a good idea."

Father Dowling had the impression Mr. Wilson was studying him out of the corner of his eye. No doubt the caretaker had vivid memories of Rosemary coming at him with a raised poker. It was difficult to know what the old man had made of that strange sight.

The shuffleboard game had come to an uneven end and the losing couple tried unsuccessfully to interest their conquerors in a rematch.

"Care to play, Father?" the woman asked. Father Dowling thought her name was Lawton but he was not sure.

"If Mr. Wilson does."

"Nope. Sorry. Don't have the time. I have to get back to work."

Such a claim in such a place drew respectful half-resentful glances. That one of them might still occupy a productive place in the greater society was uncommon, and Woodie Wilson seemed to sense the importance he had momentarily taken on. Father Dowling would have urged Wilson to play one quick game if he were not relieved to be spared the sport himself. In any case, the Lawtons were offered a chance at vindication by another couple and the moment of danger passed.

"Miss Walsh has sure had her share of visitors since the day you were there, Reverend."

"Is that so?"

Wilson nodded and looked around as if he were thinking of spitting. Father Dowling suggested a stroll on the playground.

"Apparently she misplaced her automobile."

"For heaven's sake!"

"That's what the police said, anyway. Had to worm it out of them at that. Very close-mouthed types."

"When was this?"

"Last evening. I told them I couldn't let them into the apartment unless I knew what was going on."

"They were police?"

Again Wilson nodded and turned away. This time he did spit, inexpertly. He was wiping his chin with his sleeve and avoiding Father Dowling's eye when he turned back.

"In uniform?"

"Detectives."

"How do detectives identify themselves?" Father Dowling asked, hoping his tone suggested only mild curiosity. "Do they wear badges?"

To his relief, Mr. Wilson, having cocked his head in thought, opened an interval between thumb and index finger. "They don't wear it, no. It's in a wallet sort of case they carry here." He patted his narrow chest.

"They'd found the car?"

"I guess."

"That must have been a relief to Miss Walsh."

"Who knows? She never came home."

"Are you sure?"

"They waited through the night for her." Wilson's tongue bulged his cheek and his eyes made an unseeing circuit of the horizon. "Her business, of course. I never nose into what the tenants are up to."

Father Dowling might have praised this alleged restraint but his mind was racing. Of course Rosemary could not become a permanent resident of the rectory—a sort of Cardinal Mindzenty enjoying sanctuary in an extraterritorial house—although Marie Murkin had seen no reason in the world why she could not sleep indefinitely in her sewing room while Rosemary occupied the upper room. Father Dowling had told his housekeeper only that it was imperative Rosemary not stay in her own apartment for the time being and Mrs. Murkin seemed to construct elaborate and convincing reasons for this behind her narrowed eyes. After all, she had seen this girl come often to consult the pastor and she could infer something sufficiently important to offer her asylum was afoot. Rosemary had been moved by Mrs. Murkin's generosity but was insistent she could stay elsewhere.

"With Sharon Herman," she said to Father Dowling when he had driven her to work the previous morning. "We had surgery together."

"If there's any difficulty, let me know. A motel would do if it comes to that."

"Oh, I'm sure Sharon will put me up."

"They must be upset over her father's experience."

"That's my excuse. I'll offer to come as company for her and to help in any way I can."

"Telephone me after you've talked with Sharon."

But after he had said good-by to Mr. that did not concern Father Dowling greatly until this disturbing conversation with Woodie Wilson. How easily the old man could have been convinced by Rosemary's visitors that they were detectives. Well, it was easy enough to find out if they had been.

but after he had said good-by to Mr. Wilson and was walking back to the rectory, he wondered if it would be wise to call Phil Keegan and put the question to him. It was essential to protect Rosemary from any danger that might threaten from her former companions; it was important to keep her secret from Phil Keegan. This thought brought home to him the ambiguity of the decision he had made when he told Rosemary she need not make herself known to the authorities. It was one thing to see this somewhat abstractly, in terms of faceless investigators; it was very different indeed when it became a matter of deceiving his old friend Phil Keegan. Of course there were other considerations, ones that had been suggested to him during his chats with Francis X. O'Boyle. Prison could be a dangerous place for someone genuinely interested in reforming her life, and if there was any suspicion of informing, the danger was likely to be mortal. The conclusions O'Boyle drew from this were not those Father Dowling did. O'Boyle seemed convinced that incarceration for whatever cause was a crime more heinous than any it was meant to punish. And of course Father Dowling knew what Phil Keegan thought of O'Boyle.

"Where do those guys come from, Roger? When I was young and played cops and robbers it was always clear the cops were right and the robbers wrong."

"Did you ever play the robber?"

"When I did, I knew a robber was a robber."

Keegan's elliptical point was that for O'Boyle the cops were the bad guys but, if that were true, O'Boyle was consistent enough not to wish them behind bars. Indeed, he was almost poetic in describing the life of prison guards.

"They're as much prisoners as the prisoners, Father. The whole system is barbaric. Imagine spending your life watching other men in a cage. After a while they don't know which side of the bars is the wrong one."

Father Dowling knew which side of the bars was the wrong one for Rosemary Walsh, and he decided he would speak to her before he worried about the detectives who had spent the night waiting in vain for her to return to her apartment.

"She's not here," a brisk female voice said when he rang Fox River Realty. "Who's calling, please?"

"Roger Dowling. Father Dowling."

"Yes?"

"Did Rosemary come in today?"

The woman hesitated, then seemed to

decide that his clerical status entitled him to an answer. "No, she hasn't. Are you her pastor, Father..."

"Dowling. Yes, I am."

"I'm worried about her. She didn't come in, she didn't call in. That's not like her."

"Maybe she had trouble with her car."

"Why do you say that?"

"Well, it happens, you know, and it can upset a person."

"Her car was stolen, Father."

"Stolen!"

"Oh, it's been found. The police were here."

"Did they give their names?"

"Let me see. One was named Keegan, I think."

He thanked the woman and hung up. When he turned, Marie Murkin stood staring at him, her face twisted in contrition.

"Father Dowling, I completely and utterly forgot to tell you. She was here at lunchtime yesterday. She came to the kitchen door. She wouldn't let me disturb you when I told her Captain Keegan was here."

Father Dowling went into his office and looked up the Herman address in the directory. Telephone first? He thought not.

He wanted to see Sharon when he talked to her so he could tell what kind of person she was. The fact that she and Rosemary were friends was a good sign; if they were at all alike he would not have to be overly careful in what he said. Of course, this was a girl whose father had come very close to being shot, doubtless by accident, but that only made it more harrowing. But the great hope was that he would find Rosemary herself at the Hermans.

18

From below the window, the voices of Sharon and Norman lifted to Rosemary. She preferred this cool shaded room to the sun and chlorine of the pool. She wasn't in the mood for swimming. She wasn't in the mood for Norman either, if the truth be known. Any more, apparently, than Billy Herman had been in the mood for her.

What a thing to be fretting about now, but it hurt and puzzled her. For so long she had been in the position of cooling Billy's ardor that she had unconsciously come to think of herself as a *femme fatale*, at least as far as he was concerned. So wouldn't he at least show some interest in the fact that she was a house guest?

"Let's go to a passion pit," Norman had

suggested the night before. "There's a triple monster special at the Valley Drive-In."

Sharon was game and so was Rosemary, but Billy apparently hadn't even heard the suggestion. When it was repeated he shook his head.

"I know," Norman said. "You've seen them all."

"What are they called?"

This literal-minded, unfunny Billy was a stranger. Norman directed his effervescence elsewhere and asked Mr. Herman for a survivor's account of the slaughter on the fifteenth fairway.

"Norman!" Mrs. Herman said, shocked. "A man was killed. Mr. Herman himself is lucky to be alive. It was not another monster movie."

"Frankly, it was over before I knew what was going on," Mr. Herman said. "I was thinking of my approach shot when, bing, bang, and the next thing I know I'm being grilled by detectives."

"Grilled?" Sharon frowned at what she seemed to consider linguistic excess.

"Maybe they thought you had arranged the whole thing," Norman said brightly.

"You know, businessman lets contract on rival."

Mr. Herman stared at the young man. "Aaron Leib was retired, Norman. He was scarcely a rival."

"I meant for Mrs. Herman's affections." Norman waggled his brows and stuck a piece of celery in his mouth, a poor man's Groucho.

"That's not terribly funny, Norman," Mr. Herman said.

"I think your wife is very attractive."

"Norman," Sharon suggested, "why don't you shut up?"

Rosemary found it hard to believe that Norman was a doctor who would begin interning at Cook County Hospital in a matter of weeks. He was the least serious person she had ever known; unlike Billy, there was no substance beneath the frothy exterior of Norman Sheer. The first time she met him, after he fell downstairs, he had asked without preliminary, "How did the gynecologist answer Bugs Bunny?" and only Sharon's intervention had saved her from embarrassment, a fact she appreciated only later when Sharon explained.

"What's up, Doc," she said, sighing, but

it was obvious she enjoyed being exasperated with Norman. "Never answer a direct question from Norman."

"He'll starve as a doctor."

"Don't bet on it. He intends to be a cosmetic surgeon."

Which recalled their shared experience under the knife and explained their friendship. Sharon seemed willing to pretend that Rosemary Walsh had begun life when the bandages were removed and she was completely incurious about Rosemary's pre-history; nor was she particularly forthcoming about her own past. Rosemary suspected that Sharon was putting forever behind her a sad, rebuffed, unhappy girl. It was as if the two of them were living in an unconnected present. Sharon's family. encouraged this sense of a new life.

Lying on the bed, listening to Norman's babble, Rosemary looked at the framed photograph on the wall. In it a Sharon she scarcely recognized, a pre-operation Sharon, clung smiling to the arm of an older man, the smile conferring more beauty on her than any surgeon's knife could do.

"Aaron Leib," Sharon answered when Rosemary had asked.

"You're kidding. The man who was..."

Sharon nodded. "That was taken in Israel. That's me behind the nose. It was my year on the kibbutz. Aaron was visiting."

"Aaron?" But then, Sharon called her father by his first name.

"Uh huh. You can see how vital I look. Tanned, sinewy, the new woman. Maybe he was a nose freak. He hardly looked at me after the operation." Her eyes took on a distant look. "But then he had a way of ignoring his discards. He was Biblical in his seductiveness. Aaron's rod." Sharon tossed her head. "It's a different world out there."

Rosemary waited, but that was all. It said something for the effect of her return to normalcy that she was half shocked by this casual mention of an affair with a man as old as Aaron Leib.

"Oh, come on, Rosemary. He was in his early thirties, and I was of age. Of course, he had a rented Mercedes and we tooled around for two weeks together. Tel Aviv, Jaffa, Jerusalem. Not quite the way to see the holy places. And I was flattered. Not even Norman gave me a second look in those days."

"Was he is Israel too?"

"No. Certainly not. Norman? But Aaron was nervous as a cat most of the time, and not without reason. He did a lot of good, Aaron did, but he was a bastard too. He told his wife about us and she told my father. God. How grown up we were all supposed to be. Well, you know my parents."

Last night she had felt like a wallflower at the pool party that just formed itself after Norman made a few phone calls. Mrs. Herman always sat by the pool fully dressed, smiling benevolently at the young people, but Sharon's father cannonballed off the board and then swam the length of the pool again and again, as if he were very conscious of being alive and even happier to be surrounded by youthful laughter. Rosemary recalled that scene later when, lying sleepless across the room from Sharon, she tried to imagine the romantic affair halfway around the world between Sharon and the man who had been shot dead while seated next to Mr. Herman in a golf cart.

Her own fear and confusion lifted, replaced by these distracting thoughts of her friend's past. What would Sharon's reaction be if she knew how Rosemary had been spending the year she had worked on the kibbutz? Sharon, Billy, Mr. Herman—their lives seemed to overwhelm her own and, in the dark, it was easy to believe she had overreacted when she heard those detectives speaking with Gladys.

Yet this morning she woke with no intention of going to the office. Sharon accepted this with all the indifference of a girl who had never had to work. Rosemary assumed the Hermans were wealthy on the evidence of this house, the way they lived, the fact that Mr. Herman owned his own business, the membership at the country club, all of it. Even Sharon's year in Israel had been a luxury she could afford, just as her surgery could be thought of in any terms other than its expense. Rosemary had had to borrow the money, through Father Dowling, whom she was paying back on a regular basis, suspecting he himself was the anonymous lender.

Suddenly she was aware of Father Dowling's voice below and she jumped off the bed and went to the window. He stood there, a lean figure in clerical clothes, talking with Sharon and Norman, and for once Norman seemed subdued. It was Norman's presence that brought Rosemary hurriedly downstairs and outside, as if she feared the young doctor would make some terribly off-color remark and embarrass Father Dowling.

"Rosemary," Sharon said, relieved. "You have company."

"Have you all met?"

"Why do you think I'm edging away from the pool?" Norman asked. "It's sometimes done by immersion, isn't it?"

"Only between consenting adults," Father Dowling said lightly. "What a lovely place this is."

Sharon offered to show him around the yard and Father Dowling did not seem embarrassed to be escorted over the lawn to the flower beds by a young woman clad in the briefest of bikinis. Norman accompanied them, with something of the curiosity of a man who had never before seen a Catholic priest close up. Standing on the tile, shaded by an umbrella that emerged from the center of a metal table, Rosemary had the feeling Father Dowling was giving her an opportunity to adjust to his sudden appearance here, as if he wanted to assure her she had done nothing to worry about and that nothing had happened that might endanger her.

But something had happened.

"They found your car," Father Dowling said when Sharon brought him back to Rosemary.

"Where was it?"

"Abandoned on a country road."

Norman began to hum. "The lyrics are familiar but what's the tune?"

"Hello, hello, hello," a voice called, and they turned to see Mr. Childers coming through the breezeway from the front drive. He stopped when he saw Roger Dowling.

"Am I interrupting?"

Sharon assured him he was welcome, perhaps she was glad to have someone to balance the presence of a Catholic priest. The new visitor looked inquiringly at Roger Dowling who introduced himself.

"Lionel Childers." The two men shook hands, appraising each other as they did so. Afterward, Childers looked around and his eyebrows lifted.

"I'd hoped to find Billy here," he said. "Am I in luck?"

19

Lionel Childers was a good deal more startled than he appeared when he pushed through the screen door of the breezeway and saw the priest standing there like an apparition beside the pool. The ascetic face was turned to him and something in the expression of the priest's eyes when they shook hands made Childers think he was making the mistake of his life coming here like this.

But the moment passed, the priest quickly reverted to type, which, in Lionel Childers' experience, meant Father Dowling was pleasantly inept and determined to see the sunny side of things. After all, when you make your living convincing people that death is a release, a disguised blessing, your perceptions of the real world are bound to be affected.

"I'd hoped to find Billy here," he said. "Am I in luck?"

"You sure are. He isn't here."

Childers smiled at Norman. He had noticed that this was the way Herman handled the young ass. A medical doctor, it was difficult to believe that. It was even more difficult to accept the fact that in a few years Norman would be wallowing in money, a certainty that doubtless influenced Howard Herman. A man whose wobbly business would go to his son could be pardoned for wanting financial security at almost any cost for his daughter. And a lovely girl Sharon was, too. Voluptuous. There was no other word for the taut tan flesh, the large shapely breasts, the engaging quizzical expression. Billy had said his sister had had a nose job and, if so, more power to the miracles of modern surgery.

"Did you try the plant?"

"Not yet. I was in the neighborhood."

"Are you in munitions too?" Father Dowling asked.

The question was mildly startling. Childers doubted that such frankness was encouraged in the Herman home. The euphemism of Fox River Casing was more to protect the family than a doubtfully squeamish public.

"I am a business consultant, Father."

"Ah. Here in Fox River?"

"My offices are in the Illinois Building," Childers said pleasantly. He did not feel pleasant. He detested these polite questions from a man whose knowledge of business was probably nil. Did they train the clergy to feign interest, to inquire, to extend the hand of brotherhood? Well, two could play at that bullshit.

"What's your parish, Father?"

"Saint Hilary's."

"I don't believe I've ever heard of it," Childers said with some satisfaction.

"I'm not surprised."

"It's right here in Fox River?"

"Oh, yes."

"Of course I'm not a Catholic."

"Of course?"

"I meant that a Catholic would no doubt know of Saint Hilbert's."

"Saint Hilary's. No, my parish is an obscure one, even to Catholics."

Lionel Childers could not figure out Dowling, but he decided he could not simply dismiss the man, although what the hell a Catholic priest was doing beside the Herman pool was hard to understand. Suddenly he was amused by the thought of having this simple cleric play a role in his alibi in the unlikely case that one was required of him. Childers sat down next to Sharon.

"Father Dowling isn't as presumptuous as I am, Sharon. You should ask him to be seated."

The priest smiled away the offer Sharon was thus constrained to make, excusing himself. He went away through the house with Rosemary Walsh, Sharon's moody friend.

"A bit of a surprise, finding him here."

Sharon looked at him, as if debating whether to tell him to go to hell. Had she any idea what his connection with her father was? He doubted it. She would simply enjoy the fruits of Howard Herman's labor while remaining ill-informed about its details. His relentless smile convinced her that he was to be treated like an old friend of the family.

"How do you think I feel? He just appeared. To see Rosemary."

Childers moved the back of a hand across

his forehead. "Hot."

"Would you like something to drink?"

"Some iced tea, if you have it."

"Norman, get the iced tea."

Norman went. M.D. or not, he was as dumb as Billy. Billy. Childers' eyes drifted out over the lawn.

"Did Billy tell you he'd be here?" Sharon asked.

"Yes. Yes, he did." Childers pushed back his sleeve and consulted his chronometer, a huge timepiece bristling with stems and dials and digital windows. He punched a button and the time in six digits of accuracy appeared in mauve.

"Leave a message," the returned Norman said. "We'll be here all afternoon."

The hustle? If he left there would be just the two of them here now that the Walsh girl had apparently gone off with Father Dowling. A pool, and an empty house to play house in. Ah, youth. And too damned bad about them too. The whole point of coming here was to be here when...

The sound of the ringing telephone nearly tugged Childers out of his chair, but he restrained himself. Be calm, be nonchalant. He lit a cigarette and enjoyed the sight of

Sharon Herman's rhythmic bottom as she padded barefoot into the house.

"I wouldn't mind a dip myself," Childers said, glancing toward the pool, exhaled smoke sliding from the corner of his mouth.

Norman said nothing, his eyes on the house. And then Sharon's voice was audible from within.

"Mr. Childers, it's for you."

Sighing, he rose. Business pursues successful consultant to poolside, disturbing stolen minutes of relaxation. Sharon held the screen door open for him.

"It's Daddy."

"Thank you, Sharon." As he passed her in the doorway, their eyes met and Lionel Childers sensed as he had once or twice before that Sharon did not immediately dismiss him as an impossibly older man. There was not a challenge so much as frank curiosity in her gaze. His voice was a shade deeper than normal when he picked up the phone and said hello.

"Childers?"

"Yes, Howard."

"Have you seen Billy?"

Childers glanced toward the screen door. "Why no, I haven't."

"Sharon said you were waiting there for him."

"That's right. I gather you want to see him too."

On the other end of the line, Howard Herman seemed undecided whether to go on. Childers could appreciate his reticence. Their dealings with each other had always been business and little more. After the golf course incident, Childers felt the time had come to move their relationship onto a different plane, at least briefly. He decided to help Howard Herman to make up his mind.

"Howard, the reason I want to see Billy . . ." Childers let his voice drop into a register of deep confidentiality. "I had a rather strange visit from the police a short while ago," he lied. Tuttle's call informing him that the police were looking for Billy gave him this trump to play. And it took the trick.

"Oh God, you too! Okay then, you know."

"Maybe I should come out there."

"I'd appreciate that, Lionel."

"Of course. Ten minutes."

He hung up but remained by the phone

for a moment. The cool silent house seemed to envelop him like an expensive womb. Such comfort, such opulence. The casual visitor would assume that all this belonged to Howard Herman. Lionel Childers knew otherwise. This lovely house and yard, like Fox River Casing, was mortgaged up to Howard Herman's ear lobes. It would be excessive, he decided, to covet Herman's home as well as his business. No, Lionel Childers would be content when he became, as soon he would, the owner of Fox River Casing, precisely at the time when Aaron Leib's murder wrote finis to Wilfrid Volkser's effort to block the administration's military-aid plan.

At the plant, Howard Herman all but pulled him into his inner office. "What did they ask you, Lionel?"

"The police? They came to *tell* me something."

"I know, I know." A cigar burned in the tray on Howard's desk but he took another from the humidor and began to rub it slowly in the palms of his hands. He shot a sudden look at Childers. "Why did they go to you?"

"That's just what I asked them. Of course

they never answer questions."

"Don't they?"

Lionel laughed. "Or so I'm told. What do you make of it?"

"What the hell am I supposed to make of it? My son's fingerprints found in a car abandoned near the back nine of the country club. Lionel, they are suggesting that Billy shot Aaron Leib!"

"And his own father?"

Apparently Howard had not thought of that. The police had completely unnerved him, though this was merely one more item in his regular budget of bad news. He stared at Childers and his mouth slackened, dropping open.

"Howard, sit down. There is absolutely nothing to worry about. I mean that. Did you think to ask them whose car it was they had found?"

"They said it was a stolen car."

"Nonetheless, it has an owner. The owner of record had sold it. Does the name Rosemary Walsh mean anything to you?"

"Rosemary Walsh!"

"Precisely. One of Billy's young friends. Now, isn't it a remarkable thing that his fingerprints should be found in the automobile of Rosemary Walsh? He has probably been in that car dozens of times."

When Howard Herman sank onto the leather couch, it gave off a flatulent complaint. Howard's shoulders dipped forward and a weak smile formed on his face.

"Thank God. Of course you're right."

"I hope you didn't let the police see that their suspicions actually worried you."

"Worried me!" The tenseness came back, along with a frown. Howard bit savagely at his cigar. "I threw the bastards out of here."

"You shouldn't have done that."

"Lionel." Herman sat forward on his cushion and put his hands on his knees. "Lionel, Billy talked about killing Aaron Leib. So he was joking, but he said too many times that he'd like to kill the sonofabitch. You know how he put the squeeze on us."

"I know. But nobody would have taken Billy's talk seriously."

"But he did talk."

"So did you, Howard," Lionel Childers said softly.

It was like some impenetrable experimental drama, sitting there waiting for Billy in his father's office. Howard tried to raise

207

Billy on the CB, but the bands were so crowded with freaks that the effort became an exasperating distraction. Lionel dissuaded Howard from calling the club and Billy's favorite restaurants.

"Rosemary reported her car stolen?"

"I didn't ask. She was at your home when I got there."

"Aren't her fingerprints in the car too?"

An ungallant remark, but forgivable. Howard Herman was not yet wholly at ease, though Childers' dismissal of the importance of Billy's prints in the Walsh car was decisive enough. After all, it had been Billy who had suggested the explanation. Childers' task with Billy had been considerably different.

"Billy," he told the boy, "you threatened Aaron Leib. People have heard you do it."

"Half this town has threatened Aaron Leib at one time or another."

"But they could afford to, Billy."

After he picked Billy up, they had driven out along the river, a mile or two above the marina.

"Who told you all this, anyway?"

"I have friends downtown, Billy."

To call Tuttle a friend was the sort of

exaggeration the situation called for—Tuttle and Piannoni, for the love of God. But it had given him a head start to talk with those two. He had wanted to get Billy before the police did. He had wanted to get to Billy before the police talked to Howard.

"Whose car is it?" Billy asked.

"Do you know a Gladys Horkin?"

Billy's blue eyes grew more confused. "Sure."

"Have you ridden in her car on other occasions?"

"What the hell do you mean, other occasions?"

"Were you often a passenger in Gladys Horkin's car?"

"Lionel, I was never a passenger in her car."

They stood on a bridge that arched over the river like a monochrome rainbow, silver, sparkling in the sun. "I was afraid of that."

"She sold a car to Rosemary." Billy turned, his back to the river, and folded his arms. "Are you trying to set me up, Lionel?"

It seemed only right that understanding should dawn. For Billy to have remained unaware would have removed a large part of

Childers' sense of triumph. But his victim's apprehension complicated the deed he must now perform.

Donning a patient expression, Childers dropped his package of cigarettes and stopped to retrieve it. The idea was a simple one. He would grab Billy's ankles and lever him over the railing of the bridge, counting on surprise and speed. But when he reached for Billy's ankles, he managed to grasp only one of them. He lifted that and Billy grabbed hold of the railing and began to kick at Childers with his free foot. Pain increased Childers' determination. It brought anger too. He had meant this to be an artful act, adroitly done, over in the instant it was begun. It became an undignified wrestling match, the two of them scuffling about on the gravel walk. But Childers was not to be denied. Suffering Billy's kicks, he worked with the one leg he had managed to grasp, lifting it higher and higher. It was when Billy let go of the railing in a doomed effort to seize his assailant that Childers, with a great grunting effort, achieved his goal.

He was panting and perspiring when he hung over the railing and watched Billy Herman drop twisting into the river below.

20

Cy Horvath had had trouble accepting Keegan's remark on Mrs. Leib's reaction to her late husband's infidelity. He was himself so monogamous by nature that he could not even imagine bedding a woman other than his wife—behind the Slavic impassivity of his expression beat a heart freighted with romantic fatalities as well as with the simple maxims of his moral code. No more could he imagine indifference to such activity.

"Go over and sit in divorce court for a few hours," Keegan advised.

·"So it happens. But that's it. When it does, people break up. They don't sit around being philosophical about it."

"You want to devote yourself to Aaron Leib's girl friends?"

"Not if you don't want me to."

But he knew Keegan shared his disbelief that all this casual sleeping around was accepted as on the level of a warm handshake, nor did he misunderstand Keegan's apparently reluctant go-ahead. The abandoned car still registered in Gladys Horkin's name provided his excuse.

"Lieutenant," Gladys said. "I'd love to sit and talk, but my bread depends on my working. I just don't have the time."

"I understand."

"Good."

Horvath settled into a chair in Gladys Horkin's office and took out his notebook. "I'll be as quick as I can."

"I can only give you minutes, okay?"

"You're single, right?"

"Divorced."

"How long ago was that?"

"What the hell difference does it make?"

Horvath scowled at the blank page of his notebook. "You said you were the agent when Aaron Leib bought his house?"

"I was."

"When was that?"

"I'd have to look it up."

Horvath nodded.

She said, "You really want to know?"

"I really want to know."

She said an unladylike word and went to one of the file cabinets in the corner. Horvath had the impression that she was taking more time than she needed. He doubted she even had to consult the file. "It'll be two years next December," she said over her shoulder. "Isn't this the sort of thing you can look up in records?"

"It takes more time."

"Sure, but it's your time, not mine."

"Your husband's name is Dennis Lubins?"

"My ex-husband."

"What does he do for a living?"

"He is administrative assistant to Wilfrid Volkser."

"He's not in the book. I did look that up."

"Try the District of Columbia directory."

"He lives in Washington?"

"That's right."

"Then you must have lived there too."

"More or less."

"Was that the reason your marriage broke up?"

"You might say so. But the question, Lieutenant, is why the hell should you?

What have my personal affairs got to do with anything of interest to the police?"

"I think you know."

"I think I don't. And unless you tell me, I'm going to have to ask you to go. I'm going to ask you to go anyway." She looked at her watch and her expression was theatrical. "Do you realize what time it is?"

"Mrs. Lubins, your car was found abandoned in a place near the spot from which Aaron Leib was shot."

"I am not Mrs. Lubins."

"You are not Mrs. Lubins. But you were. You also had an affair with Aaron Leib."

"Who told you that?"

"Isn't it true?"

She lit a filter cigarette, studying Horvath as she did so. "You make it sound almost sedate. An affair with Aaron Leib. It could be a song title. Did Mrs. Leib tell you this?"

"She was aware of it."

"Oh, no doubt. Aaron was far from secretive."

"I gather it wasn't at all furtive. You were his guest at the country club?"

She nodded as if excruciatingly bored.

"So you would know the set-up out there fairly well."

"Lieutenant, I don't golf. I couldn't find the fifteenth fairway if you gave me an hour's head start. I had lunch with Aaron several times at the country club, yes. I'm sure others have told you that."

"Yes."

"That was a long time ago."

"Were you still married at the time?"

"Barely."

"Mrs. Leib doesn't seem to have been bothered by her husband's affairs."

"Doesn't she?"

"No. What did your husband think?"

"Think? You flatter him. He works for a politician."

"He didn't know about it?"

"Why don't you put the question to him?"

"Did you own the Nova when you were still married?"

"I did."

"I understand it was your habit to keep a spare ignition key under the floor mat."

"I told you that."

"Your husband would have known of the habit, I suppose?"

"Lieutenant, are you suggesting that Dennis Lubins came here, took Rosemary

Walsh's car, drove out to the country club and shot Aaron Leib because I had had several lunches with the man nearly two years ago? If he were capable of something like that, why would he have waited so long?"

"Some things get worse with time rather than better."

She rose. "Lieutenant, it's really fun playing Twenty Questions with you, but time's up. I mean it. If you want to suspect Dennis Lubins, that's your business. But you're going to have to chat with him about it. We are divorced. We don't even see each other any more."

"But you saw him the other night."

She sat down. "Did he tell you that?"

"Isn't it true?"

"My God." She sat forward, as if trying to engage Horvath's eyes for the first time. "He put you up to this, didn't he? Dennis? How do you like being used by a vindictive husband? You can see why our marriage broke up. He is the most single-minded bastard I have ever known. He will never forgive me for leaving him. He is the sun, I am the moon—that is his view of marriage." She swallowed. "It's probably yours too, but don't be a sucker, Lieutenant. Dennis Lubins is trying to mix me up in Aaron Leib's death just to settle an old score."

"Then two years would not be too long?"

"For him to wait to get even, two hundred years wouldn't be too long. Don't get mad, get even. That is one political rule I learned from him."

"How would he mix you up in Leib's death?"

"My car."

"You mean, leave it out there...."

"Sure."

"But he would have to know that's a bad place for your car to be found."

"And he didn't know."

"Unless he shot Leib."

Her eyes sparked with thought, but she seemed deliberately to extinguish it. She began to shake her head slowly. "No. No, I can't believe that of Dennis. He'd be more likely to shoot me."

Was it shrewdness on her part that from the beginning had deflected his questions concerning her former husband? She herself could be called a woman scorned, and was there a statute of limitations on her grievance any more than on a rejected husband's wrath?

"You were here in the office at the time Leib was shot?"

"When was he shot?" Horvath told her and she shook her head. "Probably not."

"Where were you?"

"Not shooting Aaron Leib. I was working!"

"Rosemary Walsh would have been here though?"

"Ask her."

"Where is she?"

"I wish I knew. She's supposed to keep pests out of my hair."

He let it go. To hell with it. He remembered the taunt of his boyhood. "Does your old man work?" "No, he's a cop." Whatever he was trying to accomplish by questioning Gladys Horkin Lubins, it wasn't working. Maybe Robertson was right and he and Keegan were only being stubborn.

In the car, he checked in and received the news about the fingerprints. Billy Herman's. Horvath went back into the real estate office. Gladys stared at him in disbelief.

"Oh, please, Lieutenant."

"A question. Do you know Billy Herman?"

"Yes, I know Billy Herman."

"How?"

"The way I know you. He comes here and disrupts the office. He is making a big play for Rosemary Walsh."

"They go out?"

"They go out."

"Thanks."

"Hey, wait," she cried, before he got to the door. "Why are you asking about Billy?"

"Just routine."

"Go to hell."

Back in the car again, he called in and told them that routine had just made the presence of Billy Herman's prints in the abandoned car innocuous.

"Innocu-what?"

"He and the current owner of the car are friends. Of course his prints are in her car. It doesn't mean a thing."

"Then why did they just fish Billy Herman's body out of the Fox River, Horvath? Or is that innocuous too?"

21

When Phil Keegan sat in the rectory office with Roger Dowling, the strain of the past several days since the fishing of Billy Herman's body out of the river told on the detective's face. The case he had feared would be snatched from his hands by a federal investigation was now emphatically his and it was hard not to wish he could still believe some anonymous Arab had been hiding in the woods by the fifteenth fairway of the country club golf course. It did not help, as it often had before, to describe the current state of an investigation to Roger Dowling.

"Of course Robertson is certain it was Billy Herman," he concluded.

"Aren't you?"

"At this point, I'm certain of nothing."

"Well, two men are certainly dead."

"Yes, two men are dead and it is very convenient if one murdered the other and then committed suicide."

"Remorse?"

"Or afraid to face the music." Keegan smiled. "Face the music. Where did that phrase come from?"

But Roger Dowling had not heard. "Does Chief Robertson have a motive for young Herman?"

"Motives. Roger, I can provide motive and opportunity for three or four people. What I cannot provide is the weapon that killed Aaron Leib."

"But what would Billy Herman's motive have been?"

"Leib was an arm-twisting fund raiser who showed no mercy. Even worse, he all but accused the Hermans of aiding and abetting the assassins. There was some reason to believe that Herman had sold big to the Arabs, Leib said the PLO."

"Munitions?"

"Small-arms ammo, all of it of a military type. They are at the mercy of military-aid bills."

"But then Aaron Leib could have been a powerful lobbyist for them."

"Not when he accused Herman of supplying arms to the enemies of Israel."

"Is that true?"

"Herman tells me, and it makes sense, that he has no control over the ultimate destination of his products. He can't prove they don't end up in PLO hands. Aaron Leib threatened to have Fox River Casing cut off from any further government contracts."

"Could any of the other munitions makers satisfy Leib's demand that their material doesn't get into the hands of Israel's enemies?"

"No. No, they couldn't. But he knew Herman personally and he doesn't know the big boys. He was a great advocate of doing what you can and not worrying too much about what you can't do."

"That's a good principle."

"Not for the Hermans. Leib was turning them into pariahs in the Jewish community. And he had convinced some bankers that the Hermans would be bypassed even if the military appropriations bill makes it through Congress."

"It is hard to feel sympathy for an armaments manufacturer."

"Oh, come on, Roger. You're no pacifist."

"Hawk or dove? There are countless species of bird."

"Yeah."

Phil Keegan could feel sorry for Howard Herman. It had been cruel enough to be accused of being less than loyal to his fellow Jews, but to see the business his father had built up threatened was cruel too. Neither of those could compare with the anguish he now felt at the death of his only son. He had fallen apart when he got the news, literally. He had required medical help in his office and had been transported to his home by private ambulance. Hours had gone by before Keegan had had a chance to talk to him; in his bedroom, the shades drawn, the air chilled by a too-effective central unit in the basement, Herman lay on his back, the covers pulled to his chin. His head on the pillow looked curiously disembodied, and Keegan felt he was consulting an apparition at a seance. Where did such thoughts come from?

"It's my fault, Captain. I put him up to it."

"How do you mean?"

"He had heard me rave about Leib. I threatened to kill the bastard. He was ruining me, but I was shocked when my son uttered the same threat. Of course I thought he was like me—a talker not a doer."

"You think he killed Leib?"

Herman had not had to say it. The certainty was like a dull light in his moist eyes. The covers moved, a tremor, and an imperfectly stifled moan emerged from Herman's lips. He was crying, and his weeping was that of a man in despair.

"Did your son have a rifle?"

Apparently there was a wide selection of weapons at the plant. Keegan stepped out of the room. He wanted a complete inventory made of the firearms at Fox River Casing. Were any missing? Was there a remote chance the murder weapon had been taken from the plant and then returned there?

"Well?" Roger Dowling asked.

"There is a missing rifle. It's possible—probable—that the shots were fired from it."

"All three?"

"There were only two shots."

"At the golf course. But there was another at Cub Park."

"The condition of the slugs will make it hard to prove all three came from the same weapon. The truth is that the defense, if there were a defendant, could make hash out of the claim that the two golf-course bullets came from the same weapon."

"The defense?'

"If we should ever get this thing to trial."

"You're not convinced by the gun missing from the Herman plant?"

"A missing gun is a missing gun. Sure, it's not being there is a fact. But I'll feel a lot better when we have the damned thing."

"It may be at the bottom of the river."

"Thanks, Roger."

"Would you like another beer?"

"I'll get it," Keegan said, heaving himself to his feet. Roger had stood too, but Keegan was closer to the door.

In the kitchen, having taken a beer from the refrigerator, Keegan paused. Voices. Female voices. They were coming from behind the closed door of Mrs. Murkin's sewing room. Odd that he had never thought of the housekeeper having company of her own. He mentioned this to Roger Dowling when he was once more seated across from him.

"Did she introduce you, Phil?"

"Good Lord, I didn't disturb them."

Roger Dowling smiled and went on filling the bowl of his pipe. Roger was one of the few people Phil could imagine not minding his guests drinking when he could not. That was a topic they avoided, of course. Roger's difficulties with alcohol Keegan had to take on faith. Those difficulties were as far behind the priest as such difficulties ever get. Roger seemed content with his pipe and endless cups of coffee. Despite Mrs. Murkin's objections, he had a coffeemaker in the study and Keegan could never recall the red heating light being out.

"Tell me about your other suspects, Phil."

"All I said was that a lot of people had motive and opportunity."

He would run through his list for Roger, why not? There was nothing all that secret about it, although the newspapers, like Robertson, had already wrapped up the case. Billy Herman had killed Leib and then himself. Herman Senior had been no more reticent with the journalists than he had been with Keegan.

"What do the other Hermans say?"

"Mrs. Herman is saying nothing. Of course the daughter denies it."

"Why of course?"

"She had a much higher opinion of Billy Herman than his parents did."

"Phil, it's a sordid idea, but Howard Herman had as much motive, even more, than his son."

Keegan could not suppress a chuckle. "That would be quite a trick, shooting at himself."

"Wouldn't it? That's just what I was thinking."

"Roger, he was in the golf cart with Leib."

"I realize that. We have his word for it. He need not have pulled the trigger himself. Only arranged to have it done. It would be a very effective touch to have himself a seeming target as well."

"In a sense, he admits as much, when he says he puts his son up to it."

"But imagine, just imagine, that that isn't the way it was. Imagine the assassin was someone other than young Herman."

"Who nonetheless commits suicide because his father is such a monster?"

"If he committed suicide."

"Someone just picked him up and threw him in the river?"

"Where is he thought to have jumped from?"

"Stratton Bridge. You'll be happy to know that Cy Horvath resisted the suicide explanation too. He even thinks there are signs of a struggle on the bridge."

"What kind of signs?"

"The walkway is covered by loose gravel."

"It was disturbed?"

"No. For about ten feet it was smoothed down very carefully."

"Cy Horvath has an interesting mind," Roger Dowling said.

"The dog that didn't bark?"

Keegan settled back, sipped his beer, and listened to Roger build up the case against Howard Herman. It was always something to hear the theories the priest would weave. Half the time they seemed aimed at deflecting suspicion from the obvious suspect. Not that Roger was anxious to have anyone else nailed for a crime. He just seemed too willing to wait for the Last Judgment. Nonetheless, it was always interesting to hear the priest construct hypotheses in his calm precise voice while puffing methodically on his pipe.

"We would need someone whose interest it was to get rid of both Aaron Leib and Billy Herman."

Phil Keegan grunted. "An Arab."

"Oh, I think you're right to discount the possibility of international assassins."

"I'm not so sure I do discount it."

Dowling waved his pipe, sending up a perfect smoke ring. He watched it rise. "There are many possibilities. Take A, the assassin. He does what he has been hired to do."

"By Howard Herman?"

"Yes. Whereupon Herman's son, learning of what has happened, threatens to divulge it. The assassin is called upon to defend himself by doubling his crime."

"Howard Herman would never order the death of his own son, even granting he wanted Leib dead."

"Certainly not. And that is why he collapsed when he heard the news. He knows who did it, but the closest he can come to an admission is the vague adoption of his son's imaginary guilt."

"So all I have to do is find the hired assassin."

"I suppose you've been looking into Howard Herman's associations and his recent movements. Where was he when his son died, by the way? '

"In his office. With a business consultant."

"Not Lionel Childers?"

"How do you know of him?"

"I met him at the Herman house."

"When the devil were you at the Herman house?"

But Roger Dowling was having trouble with his pipe and began working at it with a pipe tool. When he was finished, and had relit the pipe, he had lost the thread of his theory.

"You said there were other suspects, Phil."

"I said there were others with motive and opportunity. Howard Herman, for one."

"Then you don't dismiss my wild conjectures?"

Two can play the game of logical possibility. Keegan sketched an alternative scenario. Howard Herman, leaving the golf cart to Leib and walking to his own prudent drive, took a rifle from his golf bag and shot his partner, shooting twice. Having done so, he buried the rifle in a sand trap, ran to the cart, made certain he had killed Leib, then sounded the alarm.

"The rifle was in his golf bag?"

"Why not?"

"Because his golf bag was on the cart."

"That's his story."

"Phil, a man would not remove his bag from a cart and carry it the distance Howard Herman would have had to. Besides, didn't one of the bullets strike his clubs?"

"We found the slug in the bottom of the bag, and a hole in the bag."

"Well, then."

"He stood his bag against a tree or even laid it on the ground, shot at it, carried it back to the cart and . . . You're smiling."

"The only thing that makes your fancy remotely plausible is the fact that Leib and Herman were golfing together. I would very much like to know what led two such bitter enemies to go out on the course together."

"We have only Herman's version of that."

"And a very implausible version."

"Okay. But our conversation isn't being governed by plausibility."

"It's true that Leib was a womanizer?"

Keegan nodded. His beer can was empty

and he squeezed it in his hand. That had meant something prior to the advent of the aluminum can. Before he could stop Roger, the priest had gone to the kitchen for a replacement.

"You don't have to wait for me, Roger," Keegan said, taking the fresh can of beer.

"It's the least I can do in return for your letting me in on all your professional secrets."

"Too bad you can't reciprocate."

"How do you mean?"

But Roger knew what he meant. Nobody, certainly not Phil Keegan, could expect a priest to gossip about the confidences that came his way. He said, "Yes, Leib was a ladies' man."

He gave Roger a summary of Horvath's conversation with Gladys Horkin Lubins.

"The woman who owns the stolen car?"

"Who owned it. She claims she sold it to her secretary. And she had signed the title over."

"But she could have used her old car, driven to the golf course, shot the lover who had callously shunted her aside." Roger Dowling interrupted this imaginative flight and his voice altered to a less facetious tone.

"Where was she when Leib was killed?"

"She may have been out. She may have been in her office."

"Was she?"

"She's too busy to be sure."

"Can't you find out?"

"There is a secretary."

"Who are the other suspects?" Roger asked abruptly.

"Well, I haven't spoken with the secretary. Rosemary Walsh."

"Is she the only corroboration of Gladys Lubins' alibi?"

"Alibi!"

"Forgive the Latin."

"Is that Latin?"

"Now you're pulling my leg. You say Mrs. Lubins is divorced?"

"Did I? Yes, she is. Her husband is Wilfrid Volkser's administrative assistant."

Roger Dowling looked appropriately surprised. Keegan had saved this to the last, knowing Roger would find it as tantalizing as he and Horvath had. If international politics were excluded, national politics need not be. Aaron Leib, a more than merely potential rival of Volkser, a sworn advocate of all that the incumbent opposed, is conveniently cut down on the golf course. The swift flight home by the congressman is an obvious ploy. He despised Leib in life, he could scarcely mourn him sincerely in death. That flight was the flight of a politician from whom a great burden has been lifted, rendering him lighter than air. At any rate, full of gas. Had Roger seen his arrival at O'Hare?

"Didn't we watch it here together?"

"That's right, we did."

"Did Lubins fly in with Volkser that night?"

"No. He was already in Fox River. At least, in Chicago."

"Ah. What account does he give of his time?"

"I haven't spoken with him."

"Horvath?"

"We've gone at it indirectly," Keegan said with some impatience. "It's not the sort of thing we'd want the newspapers speculating about."

"I admire your discretion."

"Robertson," Keegan growled.

"How long has it been since the Lubins were divorced?"

"Over a year."

"And neither has remarried?"

"No."

"And what of Mrs. Leib, Phil?"

What, indeed? The death of her husband had left her, at thirty-three, an extremely wealthy and attractive woman. Whatever restrictions being the wife of Aaron Leib had imposed on her existence were gone forever now and she was free to bloom as she would.

"On the other hand, Phil, one could say she has been deprived of a good deal more. After all, if Leib had been elected to Congress, her stage would have been considerably broadened. And as his wife she was already wealthy and attractive. She knew of his dalliances—"

"Yes."

"And told you she didn't care."

"You don't believe that, do you?"

"No more than you do, I'm sure. What have you learned about her?"

"Roger, nothing will satisfy you except coming downtown and reading all the reports."

"Is that an offer?"

"Let me try to summarize them for you."

But the life of Mrs. Leib had been a world

unto itself, scarcely intersecting that of her husband. Skeptical as Keegan was inclined to be of her alleged indifference to what Roger Dowling called Aaron Leib's dalliances, it was difficult not to see that her own activities were at least a distraction from her husband's shenanigans.

"What sort of activities?"

"Junior League, Ladies' Auxiliary, Red Cross, you name it. She worked harder than women who work. Something different every day, but always something demanding."

"Well. What are you two conspiring about?" Mrs. Murkin stood in the doorway.

"Are we keeping you awake?" Keegan asked apologetically.

"Not at all. Rosemary and I were just about to have some tea and I wondered if you two wanted anything."

"I have coffee," Roger Dowling said. "Phil?"

"This is all the beer I'll need," Keegan said, flourishing his can.

Encouraged by Dowling, he went on about Mrs. Leib after Mrs. Murkin left, but eventually they came back to Dennis Lubins. Roger thought it a great mistake not to have talked with the administrative assistant before his return to Washington.

"What return to Washington?"

"Do you mean he is still in Fox River."

"Roger, we do have some idea where he was at the pertinent times. Talking to him would serve no real purpose."

But even as he said it, he felt sheepish. That damned Robertson. It was a sour note to end the evening on, but he had to get home. He did not want to abuse Roger's hospitality. It meant more to him than he could have told Roger Dowling to have a friend like the pastor of St. Hilary's.

Only later, before he fell asleep, all too conscious of the amount of beer he had drunk, did he wonder who Mrs. Murkin's friend Rosemary was.

22

Lennie Miller hoped Childers would take his absence as just a way of playing it smart, though Lionel had probably meant he should not change his style of life. A good idea, Lennie couldn't agree more, but after Rita made off with the ten thousand dollars he sure as hell was not going to chalk it up to experience. He was going to find her and get that money back. But getting the money back was not as important as teaching her that no hustler pulled that kind of trick on Lennie Miller and lived to laugh about it.

Because he could imagine her laughing about it. God, what an ass he had been! How could he have been so stupid as to trust her? It hurt, really hurt, to remember how, holding her, feeling a great tenderness for her, he had told himself this was love. Well, maybe not love, but as close as you could come to loving someone like Rita.

The only extenuating fact was that it must have been done on the spur of the moment. She had wakened before he did. She had gone through his pockets, of course she had; it would have been a reflex action. Imagine that broad opening the envelope and seeing more money than she had ever seen before in her life. You couldn't blame her for deciding to take off with it.

But Lennie blamed her. So she had found the money, there were lots of other things she might have done than run. She might have decided Lennie Miller was one hell of a lot more interesting guy than she had thought. She could have waited for him to wake up, been ready with a breakfast and more of the affection he had taken with him into drunken slumber as a pleasant if somewhat confused memory. She could have snuggled up and begun to talk about travel—Las Vegas, Acapulco, San Juan, you name it—they could have had a ball. He told himself he would have allowed her to persuade him. They would have gone. Maybe not right away, but soon, as soon as going fitted in with playing it smart. Instead she had cleared out, with his money and her clothes. Had she flown off to one of the obvious legendary places to blow his money?

He had to assume she hadn't. Rita was no dope. They had talked about places like that together, daydreaming here in her bed; she would remember and figure it was too risky. Besides, for all she knew, he could afford to follow her. For all she knew, he had money besides the ten thousand. Sure he did. He had exactly two hundred and nineteen dollars.

If it hadn't been for Lionel's phone call, he might have stayed right there in her apartment. But something a lot worse than Childers finding out he had been poaching on his bird had motivated Lennie to get out of the apartment. Any broad who would steal ten thousand dollars might also call the police and tell them where Lennie Miller could be found. Or she could have reported an intruder in her apartment. Anything. She knew all he had to do was attract the attention of the police and he was in trouble that could not be simply sneered away. That would have given her all the time she needed to get away. And he would have had to telephone Childers. No, O'Boyle. He would have telephoned O'Boyle.

He had always prided himself on his mind, but he hated to have so goddam much time to think. He had lain on a bed at the YMCA, ignoring the sound of the creeps prowling the hallways, and stared at the ceiling reviewing from about fifty different angles what a stupid idiot he was. Finally he telephoned O'Boyle.

"I brought Scotch," the bearded parole officer said when he eased into the room. "Which is against the rules."

Lennie tried to look grateful even though the thought of Scotch brought back memories of retching. O'Boyle held a cloudy glass up to the light, glaring at it. He put it down and announced they would drink from the bottle. He was not fooling Lennie. Lennie knew he had been cast in the role of the Prodigal Son.

"I've been a goddam fool, O'Boyle."

"Tell me about it."

The version he gave O'Boyle left out a few things. Lennie lay in the Y, a victim of his loins, having failed to resist the advances of Childers' broad. He mentioned being robbed too, of a couple hundred bucks, but that was fortune enough for O'Boyle. The story didn't make a helluva lot of sense but by that time they were well into the bottle of Scotch and Lennie's general grievance against the world was all the springboard they needed to plunge into the murkier depths of crime and punishment. O'Boyle left what Scotch remained in the bottle. Lennie poured it down the sink.

After two days of that he decided to go back to the apartment. Why the hell not? If she had blown the whistle, the danger was past. The cops were sure not going to stake out the place. They would have no idea how interested they ought to be in Lennie Miller.

It wasn't a hell of a lot better lying on Rita's bed and staring at her ceiling, but at least he was living at her expense, if you could call it living. In the freezer he found a limited assortment of TV dinners and there was enough Scotch left to get bombed the first night he spent there. But mainly he was trying to think. It was important to believe that all he needed was time and he would discover in the cracks of the ceiling the answer to what he should do now.

When he heard the key in the lock, he rolled silently off the bed, slipped under it, and, holding his breath among the accumulated dust, really believed he had known all along she would come back. It was the key that convinced him it was Rita. It was what he had come to know of her sluttish mind when they had whispered together in her bed that told him, yes, this is just what she would do. She would be convinced he had gone off in pursuit of her and where would she be safer than in the apartment from which she had initially fled?

But he lay not even breathing and knew relief only when it became certain beyond a doubt that it was Rita. Sighting down his body, he saw her shoes between his shoes. She had checked the living room, the kitchen, and finally came into the bedroom. Lennie lay wracking his brain, trying to think if there was any visible clue to his presence, but he was sure that whatever of his she might find would seem to be there from four nights ago when they had been together.

She began to hum and a moment later there was the sound of the bathroom door closing. Lennie slid out from under the bed and resumed his position on it, lying on his back, his hands behind his head, his eyes boring into the closed bathroom door.

The sound of the shower began and Rita's hum became a song. Lennie smiled grimly. It was nice she was in such good spirits. He cleared his mind. He wanted to be thoughtlessly ready when she came out of that bathroom. He had to wait for fifteen minutes, but he did not mind. All the helpless anger that had saddled him for days was gone. Only the anger remained, and the certainty that he was going to be able to do something about it.

When the door opened, a little puff of steamy air emerged and then Rita, wrapped in a towel, a pleased preoccupied look on her face. She was halfway across the room before she noticed him.

"My God!" Her hands flew up, releasing the towel, and she stood naked to her enemy.

"Where've you been?"

"Lennie, you scared the bejesus out of me."

"I've been waiting for you."

He could see the thoughts go past her eyes like the cars of a freight train. She could not believe he had been lying there patiently for four days waiting for her to come back, but she wanted to.

"Come here."

"Do you know what time it is, Lennie?"

"No, what time is it?"

"My watch." She looked around, then started for the door. He was off the bed and grabbed her by the wrist before she had taken two steps.

"You're hurting me."

He led her to the bed, threw her down, and then, not meaning to, not wanting to, took her savagely. It was as if this was the one sure way to communicate with Rita. Afterward, his arm around her neck, more a wrestler's hold than an embrace, he said, "Where is it?"

She flicked him playfully, as if in answer, and he tightened his arm.

"The money, Rita. Ten thousand dollars. Where is it?"

"He made me give it back."

"Who?" He pushed her away and sat up. She looked up at him with the eyes of a condemned person.

"Lionel. He took it back, most of it. Nine and a half. A lousy five hundred was all he let me keep."

He realized he was shaking her violently

and she was screaming. He stopped. He made himself stop. Play it smart. She shriveled up and scooted as far away from him as the bed allowed and he let her go. His voice, when he spoke, sounded like a stranger's, even to himself.

"Tell me about it, Rita. All of it."

Listening, he knew a self-disgust that had not been approached during the previous four days. Lionel had known about him and Rita. He had actually encouraged Rita to become friendly with Lennie. It was Lionel's way of keeping tabs on his driver. When he remembered the stories Rita had told him about Childers, it was all too easy to imagine her telling Childers about him.

"He said you'd come here. He said you'd have money stolen from him. I was supposed to get it back. I didn't believe him, Lennie."

He shook his head impatiently. He didn't want any bullshit.

"You did come and we got drunk and then I looked in your pocket and there it was, just as Lionel had said." Her eyes gleamed and a look of cunning crossed her face. "I figured, what the hell, you took it from him, I'll take it from you." The

246

shrewdness was all gone now. "He was waiting for me. He must have spent hours sitting in the car down there in front of the building."

"He drove himself?"

"Lennie, he drives himself most of the time. The times you drove..."

He didn't want to hear any more what a damned fool he was, not from Rita. What he had to know was whether she had been told what really explained his having that ten grand.

"He said I stole the money?"

"Yes. Didn't you?"

She was beyond guile now, he was sure of it. Besides, he wanted to hear again how Lionel had paid her off with a measly five hundred. That is all she had gotten for betraying him. What a sucker.

"It's more than you got," she snapped, and he hit her with the back of his hand. She cowered and then, inexplicably, he reached out and tugged her to him.

"He screwed us both, Rita."

"Well, I don't know about that," she said, and it was good to hear her teasing tone again. After four days in solitary, he needed companionship, and even if he couldn't trust

Rita, she was warm and close.

"I'm going to get that bastard," he said.

"I'll help, Lennie. Together we can do it."

23

Lennie got off the bed and crossed the room, holding his arms out from his body in the manner of a much larger and much stronger guy. Where the hell had he learned that pose, Rita wondered, but she thought she knew. She could imagine little Lennie strutting around the yard in Joliet, imitating the big johns. He would have been their errand boy, the way he was Childers' errand boy.

What a kick he got out of her talking about Lionel, telling what he was like in bed, as if Lennie was any better. As if he was half as good. What did the little rooster think he was? Her face was still ablaze from the shot he'd given her. That was another difference between him and Lionel. Lionel

Childers would never strike a girl.

But by God, he had sounded as if he wanted to when she called up about the money she'd lifted from Lennie.

"You what!"

"Geez, don't tell me it isn't yours!"

Hardly a pause, and then, "It's mine. Where are you calling from?"

"You don't sound very happy about it."

"Rita, Lennie is a very dangerous man. There's no telling what he might have done to you."

That was better, much better. She told him where she was, in a bar, and he said he did not want to meet her there, but she was used to that. She had never gone out with Lionel. Talk about careful. He didn't have a wife. At least he said he didn't, and Lennie backed him up on that. What was he so worried about? It was not too goddam flattering a way to treat a girl, especially now, when she was bringing back the ten thousand Lennie had stolen from him.

"Is that what he told you?" Lionel asked.

She had gone to the intersection he named and waited for him to show up. He didn't even pull over to the curb, and when she ran out and opened the door and slid in beside him, he kept looking straight ahead, concentrating on his driving as he pulled across the intersection. While they drove along the lake, she told him the story she had had two days to construct.

Because for two days she had intended to take the bundle and go. Except that she could not quite convince herself she would get away with it. Ten thou was just too damned much money. During those two days she did not have a single drink, otherwise she might have chanced it, but for once in her life she wanted to make a clearheaded choice, so she sat sober in a hotel room and turned it over every way she could and in the end decided the best way she could use the money was to get onto another basis altogether with Lionel Childers. Any man who could be robbed of ten thousand dollars must have a helluva lot more, and Rita decided to throw in with Childers rather than go on a spree after which both Lennie and Childers would be out for her neck.

"Told me he stole it from you? Sure. I didn't imagine it was a bonus."

He smiled. Lennie's drunken answers to her questions after she had found the money in his pocket and returned to bed had made no sense. All she got out of him was how proud he was to have given the shaft to old Lionel and that had to mean he had taken the money from his boss.

"Strange he should come see you."

"Yeah."

"Have you been seeing Lennie?" For the first time he turned to look at her and she was frightened by the cold depths of his eyes.

"Are you kidding?"

"I don't own you, Rita. I can't tell you not to see someone else."

"Lionel, forget it. Why should I have anything to do with your *driver*, for Pete's sake?"

Had he believed her? She couldn't tell. But she knew enough not to keep on saying it wasn't so. She opened her purse and took out the envelope. He accepted it, slipping it almost casually into his jacket pocket.

"You're welcome," she said angrily.

"Oh, of course. Thank you, Rita."

"What the hell, it's only ten thousand. Maybe I should have let Lennie keep it. You don't need it."

He smiled. "Have you been back to your apartment?"

"Not on your life. Or mine."

"He'll figure you're long gone by now."

"I could have been. I thought about it, Lionel."

"I'm sure you did." He looked at her again. "I'm trying to understand why you didn't."

She tipped her head and made a face. His expression was blank. She moved closer to him.

"I haven't been seeing other guys, Lionel. Not since..."

He laughed. "Rita, I'm not a damned fool."

So she laughed too. Why not? "Wouldn't you like for me to stop seeing other guys?"

"That would change your whole style of life."

"It sure would."

"Let me think about it."

"What's there to think about?"

"What exactly did you have in mind?"

"Lionel, I know you want to be discreet. Okay. I've never objected to that, have I? So that's what I have in mind. I'd like to be in an apartment nearer to you, maybe in Fox River. That would be more convenient. I want to get out of the business, Lionel."

He nodded, considering. "There's a slight obstacle, Rita."

"What?"

"Lennie. I don't expect to see him again, not after this." He patted the envelope. "But you should be expecting a visit. He is going to be very angry with you."

"I know. I need protection."

"In many ways it would have been better if you had let him keep the money. I mean, with it he would have left for good."

She started to cry when she realized what he was saying. He didn't care about the money as much as he did about her. He thought ten thousand dollars was a small price to get rid of Lennie Miller and all the rest of them so she could get out of the life. Lionel soothed her. What was done was done. And she wasn't to worry about Lennie. He would take care of Lennie. An ex-con who walked off with his employer's money was in a very bad position.

"But he doesn't have the money."

"All the better," Lionel said, changing his tune. "I can still make things hot for him and he knows it. That's your protection, Rita."

He dropped her at the same intersection

at which he had picked her up. He would be in touch. The sensible thing would be for her to take that trip she had decided against. Get out of town until Lionel had an opportunity to fix Lennie Miller. "Neutralize" was the word he used.

And so she had taxied back to the apartment. In her purse was the five hundred in cash Lionel had given her, plucking the crisp bills from his wallet. Meanwhile, she would consult travel agents.

The apartment brought back the drunken night with Lennie and her hurried exit. How long had Lennie hung around? She would have bet even money he was prowling the strip at Vegas, looking for her. She began to hum. A shower. She would shower and then start making plans for the trip that was step one in her retirement.

When she came out of the bathroom and saw Lennie lying on the bed, she went cold all over, despite the fact that she still glowed from the shower. Where the hell she thought she was going when she started naked toward the door she didn't know, but then the animal was all over her and she went through the motions, hating him, wanting to claw him until he bled. And all the while her mind was searching for a half-believable lie to tell him, and then afterward he lay exhausted and she was glad his first move had been a caveman one. He wanted to know all about it and she told him and she could not believe he was believing her. He *wanted* to believe her, that was it. He had no trouble at all with the idea that she would take off with that envelope once she laid eyes on it. But turning it back to Lionel really did it.

"I'm going to get that bastard," Lennie said.

"I'll help, Lennie. Together we can do it."

24

When Keegan said, to hell with Robertson, he wanted to look into the Dennis Lubins angle, Cy Horvath nodded.

"I just want to satisfy myself there's nothing there," Keegan said.

"There are two possibilities there."

Keegan displayed his palms. "One at a time, Cy, one at a time. If it were fraud, theft, misappropriation of funds, I'd go right to Volkser. You know what Mark Twain said about politicians. But killing a possible opponent? Only in the movies. No, it's Lubins I want to know about."

"No problem."

The captain's brows lifted slightly. He demanded competence but he didn't like cockiness.

"I know a guy who works for Volkser. Chuck Howard. He was a cheerleader at Central."

He still looked like a cheerleader when Horvath met him in the Press Bar.

"What'll you have?" Chuck said, punching Horvath on the arm.

"Coke."

"Still in training?"

"And I'm on duty."

"Cy Horvath, a detective. I can still remember you tucking that ball into your gut and hitting the line."

"Some days I can still feel it."

Chuck had a Coke too. Horvath wished he had insisted on a café. Bars were generally bad places for an interview. Chuck Howard thought this was just old times and Horvath had to let him know otherwise.

"I'm working on the Aaron Leib killing, Chuck."

"What for? Let the FBI take care of it."

"Haven't you heard about Billy Herman?"

"Tell me about it."

Chuck Howard listened with a patient smile, as if the old jock were trying to impress the Washington hotshot with his job.

"We're assuming it's a local matter, Chuck, until proved otherwise. Howard Herman was in that golf cart with Leib and apparently he was shot at too. Maybe he was the target. Now his son is dead."

"They make it sound like suicide."

"Maybe it is."

"Cy, I'm not going to tell you how to do your job, but I really don't follow you. Was Howard Herman in Cub Park when the first shot was taken at Leib?"

"The shot was taken at the Israeli consul."

"Or so it seemed until Leib got it on the golf course. It's pretty obvious he was the target at the ball park too."

"That's possible, sure." Horvath sipped his Coke. "But once you put the political angle, the Israeli angle, aside, other things come up. Like the fact that Leib had all kinds of enemies."

Chuck's eyes crinkled in a smile. "Wilfrid Volkser Shoots GOP Hopeful?"

"Aaron Leib was a mattress acrobat, Chuck. It's common knowledge."

"We couldn't have used it. That's an unwritten law."

"There were husbands and fathers and

259

brothers who had plenty of reason to..."

"Don't tell me Herman has a daughter too?"

"Chuck, I'm talking about Gladys Lubins and her ex-husband."

Right away Horvath knew he had hit something. Chuck Howard wasn't smiling any more. He even turned away, picked up a black plastic ash tray from the bar, and inspected it as if he had never seen such a thing before.

"Lubins was already in Fox River when you and the congressman flew back here."

"Yes, he was. On district business."

"What business was that?"

"Cy, you have to be kidding."

"I'm not kidding."

"Then I won't kid you. I'm not going to sit here and feed your suspicions about a guy I work with."

"Because he couldn't possibly have done such a thing?"

"Shoot a man?" Chuck Howard's voice had dropped to a whisper. "He couldn't. Look, I know Dennis Lubins. I know Gladys."

"Then you know Leib was the reason for their divorce."

"He may have been the occasion, but he wasn't the reason. The divorce was years ago."

"Not even two."

" 'Nay, not so much, not two...or ere those shoes were old.' Shakespeare. It was a long time ago. And did Gladys and Leib go on doing whatever they'd been doing?"

"I don't know," Horvath admitted.

"They didn't."

"How do you know?"

"I know. I talked to her. Now, don't start jumping to conclusions. I'll be frank. The thought did cross my mind that the thought might cross somebody's mind. I had to make certain, for Volkser's sake as well as Denny's, that there was nothing there that could touch us. There isn't."

"Did Gladys tell you she and Denny had gotten together?"

"Big deal. Ex-spouses meet. Let me tell you about Dennis Lubins. He believes in monogamy, okay? He can't accept the fact that his marriage fell apart. He'd like to put it back together again. The fact that Gladys and Leib were nothing any more, hadn't been for more than a year, encouraged him. There wasn't anyone else. Okay. Why shouldn't she come back to him?"

"Why not?"

"She doesn't like Washington."

"She is a pretty independent woman."

"That's another thing. Do you know what that woman earns? Upward of seventy-five thousand a year. Selling houses. Imagine it!"

"So Lubins didn't have a chance?"

"Cy, he is willing to come back to Fox River and run Volkser's district office here. He'd do that for Gladys. This is not the kind of man who would take a pot shot at the guy Gladys hadn't seen for who knows how long. What would be the point? Hell, if he were going to kill Leib, he would have done it at the time. Believe me, Cy, you're going to have to find some other husband to fit your theory."

He hadn't really expected to get anything out of Chuck Howard. Except that he had. Another husband or father or brother. And Chuck had asked if there was a Herman daughter too. Of course there was a Herman daughter too.

In the car again, Horvath rolled down the window and thought of Keegan's tale of how he and Father Dowling had spent an evening churning up crazy scenarios for what happened on the golf course. He wondered what Sharon Herman would look like cast in the role of one of Aaron Leib's discarded mistresses.

Horvath shook his head. It was too farfetched. It was okay for Keegan and Father Dowling to while away an evening spinning nutty theories, but you couldn't just stop by the house of a man who had been shot at and whose son had committed suicide—who was probably in the depths of despair—and ask the daughter if by any chance she had ever had an affair with a recently murdered man. You couldn't if you were Cyril Horvath. He turned the key, starting the car. One wild goose chase was enough. He would go see Gladys Lubins and then report to Keegan all he hadn't found out.

"Gladys Horkin," she corrected him, her visage grim. "Lieutenant, this is becoming something very much like harassment. I have work to do. I haven't had a secretary for days and I'm losing my mind. I just do not have time to sit around and chat."

"Where is she?"

"Who?"

"Your secretary. Rosemary, isn't it?"

"Rosemary Walsh. You tell me. I got a call several days ago from some woman saying that Rosemary was indisposed and wouldn't be coming in. Indisposed! She's going to be unemployed."

"When you say 'some woman'..."

"I mean some woman. She gave her name and I didn't take it down and now I can't remember it. If I could, I would call and ask her what the hell is going on."

"Some neighbor, maybe."

"That's what I thought. But the only woman in the building is in Iowa visiting her mother or something."

"Isn't Rosemary Walsh in her apartment?"

"No."

Horvath thought about that. Rosemary Walsh was the person to whom Gladys Horkin Lubins claimed to have sold the car that had been found abandoned near the country club golf course.

"The poor kid," Gladys said, and her voice had softened. "If she had deserted me because of the Billy Herman tragedy, I could understand. Maybe that's the explanation, I don't know."

"She was close to Billy Herman?"

"Maybe not as close as Billy wanted, but close."

Horvath nodded, thinking. Billy Herman could have taken the car. Had Keegan thought of that? He put it to Gladys.

"He didn't," Gladys said. "Billy didn't take the car."

"Then who did?"

"I did."

She lit a cigarette, sighed forth smoke, then said, "Okay, I've been giving you the runaround. I lied. But this is all it was. My husband, my ex-husband, wanted to talk. I didn't want to. He insisted. Finally I said, all right, I'm showing a house out by the country club; if you want to meet me there afterward, we'll talk. I took my old car, he would recognize that, the keys to mine were in my office if Rosemary had to go somewhere, which was doubtful. Lieutenant, he met me and we went off in his car and it was an extremely difficult conversation. He wants to get back together again. I don't. Still, it's flattering to be pursued like that and when he suggested dinner, I agreed. Well, the upshot was, I forgot all about Rosemary's car and then when it was found my main concern was Rosemary."

"You told us you were here in the office that afternoon."

"I was vague about that. Give me credit."

"But you weren't. Was Rosemary?"

"Oh, come on. I'm sorry about the mystery car business, but that's the point. There is no mystery."

Except that now they were deprived of the only way to link Billy Herman to the shooting of Aaron Leib. Horvath did not explain this to the lady. He was ticked off enough at her as it was. It's always the people who are so damned busy they can't waste time talking to the police who are concealing something.

He said, "If you're worried about Rosemary Walsh, why didn't you report her missing?"

"Missing? She hasn't come to work."

"And she isn't home."

"Lieutenant, if you don't mind my saying so, you are a very male male. I am not going to pry into my secretary's private life. If she chooses to..."

Horvath got out of there. The woman was corrupt, she really was. And at her age! Good God, she was older than he was and she talked about shacking up as if it were

266

something everyone did, and if they didn't, they ought to. Denny Lubins might know politics, but he was an idiot if he thought he was missing anything because Gladys had decided to leave him. Perhaps the guy was Catholic. Then he was stuck. But there are worse things. Like having to live with Gladys.

Woodward Wilson shuffled up from his apartment with a knowing smile on his face. "I want to report a missing tenant, Officer."

"She still isn't back?"

"This is the fifth day. Better start dragging the river."

Horvath just looked at the old man. "Did you know Miss Walsh's boy friends?"

Wilson threw back his head and emitted a thin joyless laugh. "Oh, sure. She used to bring them down to get my approval before she went anywhere."

"Were there many of them?"

"I'm kidding, Officer. I don't know if she had any boy friends. The only one who ever asked for her was a priest." Again the weird laugh.

"A priest?"

"A Reverend named Dowling." Wilson grew serious. "Not a bad man, at that. He's got a sort of social center going over there at Saint Harriet's."

"Saint Hilary's."

"You know him?"

"When did he ask about Rosemary Walsh?"

Wilson didn't know exactly. Last week? He wasn't sure. He wasn't sure if he had ever met Billy Herman either. Horvath showed him a photo. Wilson studied it for a minute, working his lips.

"I'd like to help you, but..."

"It might help if you'd never seen him."

"What do you mean?"

Horvath ran his tongue between his lower teeth and lip. If Billy had not committed suicide, someone had thrown him off that bridge. Horvath was sure of it. That smoothed-over gravel made no sense. And, if someone had killed Billy and old Wilson had seen the two together...But there was no point in scaring the man. "Nothing. Thank you, Mr. Wilson."

Dowling! Well, he would leave him to Keegan.

25

What she wanted to do was just crawl away somewhere and hide and cry her eyes out, but both her parents were going that route, her father more theatrically than her mother, and Sharon was ashamed of them. Ashamed because their grief was not private enough. She wanted to conceal her own from them as well as from Norman. She wanted to just sit still, stunned, and remember Billy. It was so awful to think now of all the nice things she had meant to say to him, should have said and hadn't, and now she never could.

At least she had Norman to hang on to. At the cemetery his eyes filled with bewildered tears, but apart from that he had been someone to lean on and she could see he was as embarrassed as she was at the way her parents were carrying on. And of course her mother simply refused to believe Billy had committed suicide.

"Why, why, why?" she wailed. "There's no reason. People don't do things for no reason at all and Billy had no reason in the world to..."

She couldn't even say the word. Well, why should she? Reasons. It was quaint to believe that human actions are the consequences of reasons previously mulled over. In college, in a course on Philosophy of Mind, Sharon had examined all the main theories. She ended by thinking that the whole notion of a theory was wrong. A theory presupposed there was something to be explained, and if there was something to explain, the explanation had to be a cause, a reason. But people don't act for reasons. Reasons are what we think up later so that what we have done won't seem so silly or messy.

She used to tell herself that the reason for her affair with Aaron Leib had been the inadequacy of her own father, but what in the world did adequacy mean in such a context? As a lover? Freud forbid. She had come to accept it as something she had done in a particular setting in certain circumstances. Did Israel and the freedom and independence of her year there explain it? No. It had simply happened and then it was over and that was that.

Except that she could not forget it because she had told Billy about it, and it was a lot more difficult to reject reasons and explanations for his actions than for her own.

"That sonofabitch is twice your age," Billy had said.

"No, Billy. He isn't ten years older than I am."

"He's an old man." And then Billy's face went pale. "He did it for spite, Sharon. It was one more way to get at Dad."

"Thanks a lot."

"Sharon, be smart. This was before your nose job, right?"

"How would you like a kick in the whatchamacallit?"

Billy ignored her and she watched his thoughts pursue themselves across the freckled rotundity of his face.

"I'll kill him, Sharon. I'll kill the sonofabitch."

"Please, Billy. Not on my account. Can't you think of him as just one of my rejects?"

"Does Dad know about this?"

"Thanks to Mrs. Leib."

"You're kidding!"

Her father had told her mother and they had had a screeching hysterical exchange, and it didn't seem to matter that it had been all over between her and Aaron. They had been naughty in the Holy Land, and that was that. Her father never mentioned it, but there were times when she could feel his knowledge of her and Aaron like a third presence. It was the first thing she had thought of when the call had come about the shooting at the golf course.

"How long did this go on between you and Leib? God, that boils me. The great patriot, Israeli's right-hand man, and all he wants is a chance to bang everything on the kibbutz."

"Actually, he passed up some very attractive sheep."

Billy pushed her into the pool. Why had she told him? The fact seemed to be that she considered the episode as some kind of triumph, almost Romeo and Julietish. She knew, of course she knew, what her father thought of Aaron Leib. But Aaron had made her feel beautiful, and Billy was right, it had been before her surgery. She wished she had been able to explain that to Billy, she wished she had at least tried. But she hadn't, and now it was too late.

"I can't believe he jumped," Norman said.

"Then he was pushed."

"Or he fell. Why can't it be just an accident?"

Norman meant well and she was grateful for that so she didn't tell him of the memories that plagued her, the episodes from their past, hers and Billy's, which could now seem to have been a remote preface to what had happened. Take Rosemary Walsh. Hadn't Sharon told Billy it was suicidal to pursue Rosemary, using that very word, and when she did, hadn't she thought, that's what attracts him, he wants advance knowledge that he will fail?

"He had a head for business," Norman said.

"I guess."

"Your father was grooming him."

That made Billy sound like a horse being readied for the big race. Sharon looked at the green-blue expanse of the pool, painfully aglitter in the summer sun, and remembered

Billy swimming the length of the pool, again and again and again. And he had never lost weight. He kept on looking like the Pillsbury doughboy no matter what he did.

Cute.

Dead.

Her eyes filled with tears and she blinked and that made them run down her cheeks where they dried like perspiration in the summer heat.

"There's something I'm going to have to speak to your father about eventually, Sharon. I only hope he already knows about it."

"About what?"

"I lent Billy some money. Quite a lot of money."

Sharon pushed up her sunglasses and stared at Norman. Is that all he could think of at a time like this—money?

"Don't worry about it, Norman." She reached under her chair for her purse and plunked it in her lap. "I'll pay you back. How much was it?"

"I said it was a lot."

"Goddam it, I'll write you a check. I don't want you worrying about getting your money back."

"Sharon, it was ten thousand dollars."

"What?"

"Shh." He glanced toward the house, at the drawn drapes that made the windows look so blank. "Billy said it was for your father and I could understand that your father..."

"Ten thousand dollars! You just handed Billy ten thousand dollars?"

"Let me tell you, it was a hell of a lot more difficult than that. I've got these municipals my uncle gave me, not all of them New York City, and he made me promise to hold onto them until he said it was all right to sell."

"You cashed them in?"

"The stupid broker refused at first. He said he had an obligation to my uncle. I actually consulted a lawyer to see how I could force a broker to do his business, which was to raise the money for me without telling my uncle."

"And then you handed the cash to Billy?"

"He gave me a receipt. Thank God. I didn't want it at the time. How was I to know he would..."

"Let me see it."

"Now?"

275

"Do you have it with you?"

"I think so." Norman rolled onto his side and slid a wallet from the back pocket of his hacked-off Levis. The paper was stuck behind a photo of Sharon.

"Is that your Herman file?"

But Norman was solemn when he handed her the note. "Rec'd from Norman Sheer 10,000 (ten thousand) dollars, June 15, 1979, William T. Herman." William T. Sharon wanted to cry again. Her brother borrowing money from Norman! How could he have done it?

"That was when?" she said. "A week ago?"

"Something like that."

"You'll get it back, Norman. Norman!" Sharon sat forward and her flesh coming unstuck from the chair sounded like punctuation. "Norman, what if he was robbed? I mean, my God, talk about a motive, all that money. People are strangled for a fraction of that amount."

"Do you think he was carrying it around with him?"

"I don't find that any harder to believe than that you lent him so much money."

"But it was for your father. He would

have given it to him."

He could have, but Sharon was certain he hadn't. She did not want it to be true. If Billy had been robbed, if all that money was missing, then her mother would have some basis for rejecting the verdict of suicide, if that is what the coroner finally called it. And he would, he would. But how could she go inside and confront her father? Did Billy give you the ten thousand dollars he borrowed from Norman? There had to be an easier way.

And there was. Mr. Childers. She would ask Lionel Childers if he knew anything about the loan.

26

On the way to the rectory, seething, Phil
Keegan had rehearsed what he would say to
Roger Dowling. This had been one hell of a
way to treat an old friend and so far as he
could see there was not the slightest
justification of it. Keeping a confidence? But
that didn't require making a fool of your
friends.

He had cooled somewhat when he got to
the house. The truth was he did not want to
risk losing Roger's friendship, no matter
how the priest had treated him. Turn the
other cheek? God, that was annoying advice
when it applied. Phil asked Roger to sit in
on his interrogation of Rosemary Walsh.

"Couldn't you use a gentler word, Phil?"

"Right now, Roger, there are a lot of

words I could use, but I won't. It's pretty hard to take, you know, that girl being hidden away here at St. Hilary's rectory."

"She has been a guest of Mrs. Murkin, Phil. I've explained that. Good heavens, you have been in the house while the girl has been staying with us. I'm sure Mrs. Murkin must have mentioned her in your presence."

"Okay, okay. You're innocent as the driven snow." Keegan snorted. "Now, what has the girl done? That's what I want to know. You wouldn't go to all this trouble unless you thought she needed protection."

"Certainly she needs protection. Her car was seemingly stolen, the father of a girl friend was shot at... She's a very nervous girl."

"All girls are nervous when it suits their purpose."

But Rosemary Walsh did not strike Phil Keegan as a trembling, frightened female. She was strong. There was even a toughness in her, just beneath the surface, that he associated with people wholly different from herself.

"Billy Herman was your boy friend?"

"He was the brother of a friend of mine."

"Sharon Herman."

"Yes."

"But you did go out with Billy, didn't you?"

"Very infrequently."

"We understand it was his habit to drop by Fox River Realty to see you. Rosemary, the point is this. You knew Billy Herman, probably as well as anyone. I want you to think of anything he said or did that would have led you to believe, or leads you to believe now, that he intended—" Keegan paused—"to kill himself."

"No."

"Don't be so quick to answer. I asked you to think. This is very important."

"Is it certain he killed himself?"

"Don't you think he did?"

"I don't know. It's such an awful thought, is all. Billy was a very happy-go-lucky sort of man, full of jokes. There was nothing brooding or melancholy about him."

"He worked for his father?"

"He was vice-president of Fox River Casing. His father is president. He didn't like it when people said he worked for his father. He worked for himself, that's how he saw it. Eventually, the company would be his." Her voice trailed away as if she had suddenly been struck by the thinness of Billy's hopes.

"So he talked with you about the company?"

"He mentioned it. We didn't talk about it."

"Do you know what Fox River Casing manufactures?"

Her eyes held his and again Keegan was surprised. "Cartridges. Small-arms ammunition."

"Did Billy ever take you there?"

"Once."

"Tell me about it."

"The plant?"

"Your visit to it."

She might have been a schoolgirl reciting if her eyes had not stared so unblinkingly at him. When she mentioned the firing range, he stopped her.

"What day of the week was this?"

"A Sunday."

"And the range was being used?"

"Yes. By some off-duty policemen. Billy said they sponsored a pistol team and most of the members were police." When Keegan said nothing, she asked, "Isn't that true?"

"It's true. Did you watch them shoot?"

"We shot too."

"You and Billy?"

"That's right."

Keegan was surprised that she was so forthcoming. Not that he needed her testimony to establish that Billy Herman was an expert shot in half a dozen weapons.

"Okay, Rosemary. I want you to think about Billy there on the firing range at Fox River Casing. Did he ever in your presence make threats on the life of Aaron Leib?"

"No, he didn't."

"Didn't it ever cross your mind that Billy might have been the one who took your car from its parking place, drove to the country club, and shot Aaron Leib?"

Roger Dowling, who had been sitting behind his desk puffing meditatively on his pipe, now removed it from his mouth. "Haven't you already accounted for the car's being there, Phil?"

Keegan glared at the priest. To Rosemary he said, "I'm trying to discover what someone who knew Billy Herman thought him capable of."

"I think most of us are capable of almost anything, Captain."

Keegan lit a cigarette. The voice was the

voice of Rosemary, but the words might have come from Roger Dowling. The damnable thing was that they were true. Keegan was more skeptical of the notion of a criminal type than Roger Dowling was, but he wanted Rosemary to recall some word or deed that might connect Billy with the shooting of Leib, some memory that could provide a clue to where more solid evidence might be found. But what he really wanted was the rifle with which Leib had been killed.

"Captain," Rosemary said, "if you think Billy did it, does it matter? Even if you could prove he did it, what difference would it make now? He's dead. He's beyond investigation now."

Another Dowlingesque remark. Roger would have been here even if he hadn't been here, the way this girl seemed to have picked up his outlook.

"If we can prove he did it, that excludes the possibility someone else was responsible. No, we can't indict a dead man, but I don't want to think someone still alive is guilty and going unpunished."

"Why would Billy have shot Aaron Leib?"

"He had a number of reasons."

"I don't know what they were."

"Who were his other friends, Rosemary?"

"Friends? The few times I went out with Billy, Sharon and her boy friend came along."

"Norman Sheer?"

She nodded. "Sharon would be able to tell you about his friends. He did come by the office a lot, but he came alone and we just sort of kidded back and forth. At the Herman house, apart from the family, I met only Norman. Of course there were business associates too."

"For example."

"I don't know. I want to be helpful, but wouldn't his father know such things better than I would? I did meet a Mr. Childers at the Hermans, but I think he was Mr. Herman's friend, not Billy's."

"Lionel Childers?"

"I don't remember his first name."

"Did you go to the funeral?"

"Yes." Her eyes dropped.

"Are you a native of Fox River, Rosemary?"

"No. I come from Detroit."

"I can vouch for her since her arrival

here, Phil. It's been over a year since we met, hasn't it, Rosemary?"

"Yes, Father."

"Did I say she needed vouching for?" Keegan grumbled. "You should let the caretaker of your building know where you are, Rosemary. He's worried about you."

When she smiled, her eyes matched her face. She said she would phone Mr. Wilson. Keegan let her go. If she had been the confidante of Billy Herman he hoped she was, she was not going to tell him anything he didn't already know. After the door closed behind her, Roger Dowling suggested pinochle.

"All right. You know, I still can't get used to the idea that you've turned your rectory into a boardinghouse."

"Because I haven't. She's right, you know, Phil. Proving Billy Herman killed Aaron Leib, even if you could do it, would be a lot easier than proving he didn't."

"Did she say that?"

"I thought she implied it. Proving a negative is a mare's nest. I remember applications for annulment based on claims of non-consummation." A look of genuine pain flickered across the priest's face. Roger

285

still bore the burden of his years on the ecclesiastical marriage court.

"He did it, Roger."

"If you can put that in your files as only probable, can't you close them?"

"Shuffle the cards, Roger."

"You're satisfied now that terrorists aren't involved?"

"There's no sign of them."

"But those phone calls? Anne and Archie?"

"That's all. Phone calls. Roger, we get all sorts of phone calls. Only some of them interest the newspapers."

"Callers who claim to have killed Aaron Leib?"

Keegan fanned his cards, a cigarette in the corner of his mouth, its smarting stream of smoke rising to his eye. "That and accusing others."

"Such as?"

"Nazis from Paraguay did it. Wilfrid Volkser ordered it done. Now there's one rumor the newspapers won't touch."

"Aaron Leib's death seems to have dulled Volkser's effort to ban the sale of arms to Israel."

"Or to anyone else, Roger. Give the guy

credit." Keegan studied his cards. "Did Rosemary ever say anything to you that could help us, Roger?"

"Yes. Yes, she did."

"What?"

Roger Dowling sat back, looking thoughtful. "How did she put it? 'Anyone is capable of anything.' I think that's right."

"Thanks a lot, Roger."

27

When a plan so carefully laid comes to fruition, it is necessary to ease it to the desired climax. Haste now, after so much had gone so well, would be fatal, and Lionel Childers did not intend to lose Fox River Casing when it was almost in his grasp. Aaron Leib's death had taken the wind out of Wilfrid Volkser's sails, thus—as he had explained to Billy—killing two birds with one stone. It would have been preferable to permit Aaron Leib to be remembered as a martyr in the cause of Israel, but this had not worked out. Billy Herman bungled it when his shot went wide at Cub Park.

"Windage," Billy had complained. "I didn't take the wind sufficiently into account."

"No, Billy. Emotion. You are too heavily involved. We want a professional."

When a freckled face goes pale it is paler than most. It was the thought of the ten thousand required that stymied Billy. The Hermans, *père et fils*, had problems of liquidity and there, alas, is one of the perils of the non-public company. Family enterprises are doomed in the current economy. Look at agriculture. Lionel Childers had looked at agriculture and was reaping the advantages of having done so. His empire, like so many others, would be built on guns and butter. It had never occurred to Howard Herman that it was only by issuing stock that he could raise the kind of money needed to expand Fox River Casing to the point where a takeover by one of the giants was feasible. In the meantime, one could feather one's own nest at the undiscoverable expense of the rejuvenated corporation. But the Hermans had been in a squeeze too long to dream dreams. Both father and son wore the worried look that is a red flag to bankers, though the bank that could not see that the future of the munitions industry was as rosy as can be had Lionel Childers' contempt. It pleased him to think Norman's ten thousand dollars would provide the basis for the first transfer of stock in Fox River Casing Inc. to Lionel Childers. By assuming responsibility for the debt he would lift a weight from Howard Herman's shoulders and, since Norman in his generosity had made the loan interest-free and without provisions for a schedule of repayment—ah, the blindness of friendship—this was not a debt over which Lionel Childers need lose any sleep.

"I don't have ten thousand dollars," Billy had said.

"I know you don't. Borrow it."

"Is that the offer of a loan?"

"I don't think that would be wise, Billy. No, the money must not come from me. I have to protect myself."

Billy shook his head. "No one will lend me that much money. I'm going to do it myself."

"I will forget I heard that. I have already forgotten the incident at the ball park. It was inspired, incidentally, to claim credit in the name of Anne and Archie."

"I thought I got him."

"The consul?" Childers asked sweetly.

"No. Leib."

"Emotion. When you want something too

much, and show it, it will be withheld. I should think your experience with women would have taught you that."

"And with lenders?"

"Billy, the money is as good as yours. Think. Who do you know who can easily afford to hand you ten thousand dollars with no strings attached? Present company excluded, of course."

"I don't know anyone who would do that."

"Ah, but you do. Norman Sheer."

The idea was clearly as new to Billy as could be. His freckles were once more sustained by a healthy support of ruddy flesh. Billy began to nod.

Apart from the money, Billy must also supply the weapon. The rifle he had used unsuccessfully, one taken from the firing range at the plant, was still in the trunk of Billy's car. Lionel admonished Billy for this recklessness, but he could have hugged the young man for his lack of guile. But then, who would ever suspect Billy Herman of having taken the shot at the Israeli consul's box?

"You know who I was shooting at."

Thus the play began, written and directed

by Lionel Childers. Lennie proved to be a far better marksman than Billy, although Billy was the holder of many trophies. For Lennie it was a job, an opportunity. Lennie was ambitious. He had proved that when he had the gall to make a play for Rita. Rita had been surprised when her benefactor was more amused than angry to hear this.

"Go along with him."

"Are you serious?"

It was always well to know something about someone without it being known that one knew. Lennie's vulnerability as an alumnus of Joliet had appealed to Lionel Childers. He did have a genuine curiosity about the life of those who, unlike himself, failed to succeed in enterprises that, when they fail, are labeled crimes. How easy it was to imagine the place, prompted by Lennie's reminiscing. Lionel Childers was particularly intrigued by Lennie's tales of convicts who were regarded by the others as smart, as master minds. That they were behind bars might have been thought to count against their claim to intelligence, but not at all. There is an odd fatalism in the loser. In his heart of hearts, he expects to be caught.

This theory, after several nervous days,

had been proved again in the case of Rita. How easily her unscheduled and unforeseen discovery of that money could have destroyed the whole plan. Childers had urged Lennie to play it smart. He had meant that he should remain in Fox River and continue to come to work. He should have foreseen that Lennie would seek solace with Rita. But would even he have been able to guess Lennie would go to her not only drunk but with an envelope full of cash in his pocket, thus giving Rita the opportunity of a lifetime?

But Rita had been unable to see herself playing a winning role. After anguishing for two days, she had telephoned Lionel Childers.

He did not like it. Nor had he liked Rita's cheeky proposition that he move her to Fox River and become her exclusive source of income, but no matter. That could be taken care of at leisure in the future. It was important to cement their alliance until he had Lennie Miller once more under control. The mystery of Lennie's silence had been solved when he learned Rita had taken the envelope. What a fool poor Lennie must feel himself to be. How he would hate Rita and, having killed once, he would doubtless lust to kill her. Where was he? Where was Rita?

These questions had to be transposed into a key of stupidity in order to receive answers that would be helpful. Having imagined the unwisest place for either to be, he drove to Rita's apartment, to within some blocks of it, that is, and, strolling past, found Lennie's car parked almost at Rita's door. Had Lennie ever left the place? Remembering Billy Herman's indiscretion, Lionel opened the trunk of Lennie's car. The rifle lay there, only imperfectly concealed by a burlap bag. If only Rita had left the money alone. But then, if she had...No. He was determined to do this as he had planned. For the moment it sufficed to know where Lennie was. It was time to introduce other factors.

The bearded O'Boyle looked up with a frown and then comically struggled to rise and greet his unexpected guest.

"Mr. Childers, how are you? You should have let me know you were coming. Here, let me get some of those things off that chair." O'Boyle took an armful of papers and pamphlets and dropped them in a corner of his office. He thrust a hand at

Childers, who shook it. "This place is a bit of a mess."

"You look overworked."

"I love it," O'Boyle said enthusiastically, and Childers felt an enormous weariness contemplating the young man's idealistic countenance.

"I'm sure you do."

"Well, what can I do for you?" The frown returned and O'Boyle again looked like a revolutionary. "Is anything wrong?"

"I'm not sure. But I felt I ought to come to you."

"Lennie," O'Boyle said, and he could not keep despair from his voice.

"It may be nothing at all, Mr. O'Boyle."

"Frank."

"Frank." Did the ass intend to call him Lionel? "Let me just state the few facts I have and then we can discuss them."

Fact one was that Lennie had failed to report to work for several days. "Not in itself important, perhaps."

"The hell it isn't. He knows what an opportunity it is, working for you. I warned him not to jeopardize it."

It was necessary to interrupt. O'Boyle seemed to think of Lennie's delinquency as a high crime. But then that bode well for the sequel.

"Fact two. A young man named Billy Herman died several days ago."

O'Boyle nodded. "I read about it. A suicide."

"That's what the newspaper accounts suggest. Billy Herman was a friend of mine."

"I'm sorry."

"Perhaps 'friend' is a little strong. He is connected with a firm for which I have done work. That is how Lennie came to meet him."

"Lennie?"

"I share your surprise. One would have said the two men had nothing in common except their age. Billy Herman came from a wealthy family, whereas Lennie...But you know about Lennie."

O'Boyle's frown deepened. "His early life was hell."

"In any case, Lennie and Billy became quite close friends. I am going only on their chumminess in my offices. Frankly, I was surprised when Billy came by to speak to Lennie rather than with me." Childers chuckled. "If it had been anyone but

Lennie, I would have suspected him of trying to steal a client." Childers grew serious again. "And then Billy Herman died in rather remarkable circumstances. A young man with the world before him, bright, well liked, destined to inherit a thriving family concern, is found in the Fox River. The verdict was that he had committed suicide."

"But you don't think so?"

"I have never known anyone who committed suicide, so I scarcely qualify as an expert. By normal calculations, as I have said, Billy had everything to live for." Childers paused. "I have not seen Lennie since young Herman's death."

"What are you suggesting?"

"I don't know. I have no idea. But you can see the predicament I am in. The police are anxious to talk with anyone who could conceivably supply evidence of Billy Herman's disposition and mood prior to the time of his death. I had assumed someone else would mention Lennie Miller as a source. No one has. Nor have I done so."

O'Boyle was nodding vigorously. "Good. Good. Mr. Childers, I am positive Lennie had nothing to do with Billy Herman's death."

"But he might be able to tell the police something useful."

"What could he know that others don't?"

Childers lifted his hands helplessly. "I can't answer that. As I say, the two young men had become close. My question to you is this. Am I justified in keeping silent? I realize Lennie is very reluctant to have anything to do with the police."

"You're justified, Mr. Childers. Believe me, you are. And you're right about the police too. They wouldn't treat Lennie Miller as just a possible source of information. If there is any question at all that Herman committed suicide and they found that someone with Lennie's record had been palsy with him, well...I won't say they would frame Lennie, but..."

Childers looked appropriately shocked. "In that case, I'm glad I've kept quiet. Frank, thank you. You've taken a great burden from my mind. If only Lennie hadn't disappeared."

"I'll find him," O'Boyle said. "I know that guy. I'll track him down."

"Don't do that."

"Why?"

"I don't want him to think I distrust him.

If you and I are right, and I think we are, he'll be back and with a perfectly good explanation. This is my very first complaint about him."

"Mr. Childers, I wish more people had your sympathy."

O'Boyle came with him to the door, side-stepping piles of debris as he did so. He came out into the hall too and would have accompanied Childers to his car if a third farewell handshake had not written finis to the interview. Come to plant a seed, Lionel Childers felt he had sown a veritable crop.

And then that afternoon Rita telephoned.

"He was here when I came back." She spoke in a shocked whisper.

"Back where?"

"My apartment."

"Where is he now?"

"Taking a shower. He can't hear."

"I hope not."

"Lionel, listen. I told him you took the money away from me. I stole it and you took it. Now he's mad at you, not me. He's going to try to ... I don't know. He's really mad."

"I understand. He considers the two of you allies?"

"Yes!" She made the word resonate with her incredulity.

"Then that's what you are. Try to keep me informed. In any case, I am warned. I won't forget that."

"I'm frightened."

"Poor girl. I wish...But you mustn't remain on the phone. He is a very cunning man."

"You're telling me."

"Good-by, Rita."

"Good-by, honey."

The endearment hummed in his ear and he shivered with distaste as he hung up the phone. Lennie and Rita allies. Amusing as this was, he could not permit the charade to continue. He had need of Lennie, more now than ever after having talked with O'Boyle. Childers stood, an idea forming in his mind. But it was an idea he was prevented from executing. To his total surprise, Sharon Herman was announced, come to ask his advice about an extraordinary thing she had just learned from Norman Sheer.

28

Rita clung to him like cloth when it was time to go, hugging him, insisting she was coming along, although he told her that was absolutely out. He didn't want her or anyone else around when he had his final conversation with Lionel Childers. That was why, after driving to Fox River, Lennie waited until after five before going to Childers' building. He could drive right into the basement garage, claim his regular place, and take the elevator up to Childers' suite. Either he was in or he was out. If he was out, Lennie would wait. He would wait there with the rifle that had killed Aaron Leib. That should be enough to persuade Lionel to hand over the ten thousand and any other cash he had on hand. After, he would put the rifle to the use for which it had been made. If he was lucky, it would look like suicide, but he really didn't give a damn. The newspapers had not yet put two and two together, but they would, sooner or later. Certainly the cops would. Billy Herman, the sharpshooter. To find a rifle traceable to him via Fox River Casing next to the dead body of Lionel Childers would really give them something to think about. And it wouldn't be Lennie Miller. What the hell would Lennie Miller know about high finance and Aaron Leib and all the rest of it? The cops would be satisfied if they could account for both Aaron Leib and Billy Herman, and that would leave Lennie free to enjoy his well-earned bundle with Rita.

Rita. Seated in his parked car, Lennie pressed the back of his hand against his mouth, as if he could evoke the feel of Rita's lips. God, he was acting like a kid. Well, why the hell not? When had he ever acted like a kid when he was a kid? Ask O'Boyle. He hadn't had the chance.

The thought of O'Boyle awakened a mild worry. What the hell had he told the parole officer the night they got drunk together? He did not want O'Boyle putting that session and their session in the Y back to back and trying to figure out a connection. The one thing O'Boyle had to remember, if it came to that, was that he and Lennie had been sitting in his house drinking Scotch the night Aaron Leib was shot. At the very time. O'Boyle would swear to that. He would probably really believe it. It was almost frightening to have someone who believed so easily. But it was the sense of his own shrewdness that Lennie cherished. That made him confident about what lay ahead of him.

At ten after five he pulled away from the curb and headed for Childers' building. He got caught in traffic and it took longer than he had expected to get to the garage ramp, but it didn't matter. He had all the time in the world. If Childers was thinking of him at all, he would imagine Lennie holed up somewhere still smarting from the fact that he had let a hooker run off with the biggest wad he had ever earned.

Slipping into the gloom of the garage from the bright sunlight outside momentarily blinded Lennie, but he knew this garage like the back of his hand. The back of his hand. Rita. He wiped the thought away. No time for kid stuff now.

He put his car in its place and got out, easing the door shut as if it mattered whether he made any noise. He was grinning when he went around back to the trunk.

"I've been expecting you, Lennie."

Lennie wheeled to see Childers standing there, his arms crossed, a sad smile on his face. Lennie hadn't planned on this but he was suddenly filled with rage. Here was the bastard who had played him for a patsy. He turned and groped for the trunk lock with the key. Lionel came up beside him and leaned on the trunk.

"Wait, Lennie. Don't you understand? I've been *expecting* you. Can't you figure out why?"

"You're damned right I can. You knew I'd come for it sooner or later."

"For your money? Of course. And so, expecting that, I lurk down here in the garage day and night? Get smart, Lennie."

"Don't worry. I have." But Childers' manner unnerved him. He didn't seem worried. And what the hell *had* he been doing down there in the garage?

"Rita called me, Lennie. She called to tell me you were on your way."

"That's a lie!"

Childers did not reply. He just stood there waiting for it to seep in. Lennie could almost feel the soft ache he had nurtured while waiting in his car dissolve within him. He remembered her body pressed tightly against his, her insistence that she would come along with him to Childers. That was a demand she had counted on him to refuse. He seemed to know that now.

"Never trust a hooker, Lennie. That's a rule I would have expected you to teach me. Here."

Childers held out an envelope.

"Your money, Lennie. She stole it from you and brought it to me. Take it."

He took it. Lionel insisted he count it but a glance at the bills inside the envelope was enough. Lennie shoved the envelope into his pocket. What now? He had lost control of the situation. Rita had betrayed him. Of course she had, what the hell did he expect? Remember the terror on her face when she came out of the bathroom and saw him lying on the bed?

"Let's go upstairs, Lennie."

Childers started for the elevator and Lennie followed. There didn't seem to be anything else for him to do.

Upstairs, Lionel waved him to a chair and opened the bar. "What would you like, Scotch?"

"No. I'd like a beer. If you have any."

He felt deflated. There was no longer any reason to pretend to likes that were not his. To hell with Scotch. He was a beer drinker. Even Rita had been above him, at least she must have thought so. He patted the envelope, seeking reassurance from the feel of all that money. At least he had his money back. Childers came across the room and handed him a glass of beer. Childers himself was drinking Scotch.

"She won a few tricks, Lennie, but you have the last laugh."

"Yeah."

"Cheers."

He lifted his glass in a half-mocking salute, then brought it to his mouth. He was very thirsty suddenly. He chugalugged the glass, twelve ounces, that's the kind of guy he was, goddam it, there was no use pretending otherwise. Childers looked on with approval but Lennie wished he was drinking with O'Boyle. O'Boyle was ... what the hell was O'Boyle? A blurred Childers came and took the glass from his hand. Dizziness swept over Lennie. When he got to his feet he managed to take one step before plummeting into the dark.

Lionel Childers stepped aside so as not to arrest his fall.

29

Not even the neatness of the thing could disturb Phil Keegan's sense of satisfaction, and Father Dowling, watching his good friend doing more than justice to the eggplant casserole Mrs. Murkin had served them, was not inclined to deny Phil his triumph. Not that he wasn't curious about a thing or two.

"Roger, it only shows to go you. More often than not these things just take care of themselves."

"I don't think the police are quite that superfluous, Phil."

"We're not completely useless, no." Keegan was distracted by Mrs. Murkin coming in with her version of cannelloni. "What's this? More?"

"Now, I'm not all that sure of myself when it comes to Italian food," Mrs. Murkin said, and her tone was not unlike the triumphant one of Phil Keegan. "I have to rely too much on the book to feel right about it."

"Don't be making apologies for your cooking, Marie Murkin. Nor for going by the book. Going by the book is the better part of living."

"Phil, you should have been a preacher."

Roger Dowling was almost immediately sorry he had said that. Years ago Phil Keegan had tried his vocation to the priesthood and found it wanting and, despite a happy and successful life as a policeman, he was still far too inclined to remember the "good old days" and to wonder what it would have been like if. This speculation, given the fact that Phil was a widower, did not run the risk of hurting anyone's feelings, but Roger Dowling found it embarrassing, not least because he could discover in himself a strain of the same tendency. The past was a more comfortable place than the present and would doubtless seem increasingly so as they got older.

"And I should have been a detective, Phil.

I'm surprised you're not more suspicious of the way the body was served up to you."

"The body?" Marie Murkin stopped in the doorway, her eyes asparkle.

"We've found the man who shot Aaron Leib and in all likelihood pushed Billy Herman off the Stratton Bridge. Have you been keeping up with that news?"

"Oh yes."

"The man we found is dead too."

"Ohhh." Mrs. Murkin shook her head. "That's a shame."

Roger Dowling wondered if she was lamenting the death of Lennie Miller or the fact that Phil Keegan did not have a live killer to hand over to the district attorney. Or was she just sorry to see the end of a case that had been titillating readers of the *Fox River Messenger* for several weeks?

Phil wiped his mouth with his napkin while casting covetous looks at the cannelloni. "Suicide or accident, it's hard to say. Carbon monoxide poisoning."

Marie dutifully covered her mouth with her hand and widened her eyes. It seemed as good an exit line as any, but Marie Murkin lingered. Roger Dowling suggested she bring Phil a beer. Phil drank beer with every kind of food. Marie scurried out.

"I suppose there was an autopsy?"

"Of course."

"Nothing interesting?"

"That depends. He had taken a heavy dose of tranquilizers. That's not unusual. I suppose it made sitting inside the car in that garage with the motor running easier to do."

"Isn't the garage under that building a large one?"

"It's pretty big. The car was still running in the morning when he was discovered. He could have been there all night."

"But why there?"

"What do you mean?"

"Why in that building?"

"He had a parking place there. He worked for a firm in the building."

"Doing what?"

"He was a driver. A chauffeur. For Lionel Childers. That's what ties him to Billy Herman. The Hermans were clients of Lionel Childers, Billy Herman was frequently in the office, he got to know Lennie."

And with that everything fell into place. Given the attitude of the Hermans toward Aaron Leib, it was not inconceivable they would hire someone to get rid of their nemesis. Not they. Only Billy. There seemed no reason to involve Howard Herman, given the rest of the facts. Billy, having made contact with a man capable of killing, supplied the weapon and the money.

"Wasn't that pretty dumb, handing the man a rifle from his own plant?"

"I don't know, Roger. Suppose the idea was that the rifle would be returned to its usual place immediately after the shooting. Don't forget, they were trying to pin all this on terrorists. The percentages of our checking out every rifle at the Fox River Casing range were pretty slim. We might never have even thought of that firing range. Obviously, something slipped up."

"And Lennie Miller kept the rifle, in the trunk of his car, all this time. Why would he do that?"

Phil shrugged. "Who knows? We haven't had much luck tracing his movements from the time of Leib's death. Apparently he spent a couple of nights in the Chicago Y. The identification is pretty sure. An odd thing. He signed the register Lionel Miller."

"Could Lennie be a diminutive of Lionel?"

"No, he's a Leonard all right. After he left the Y, nothing. But we can place him on the Stratton Bridge."

"How do you do that?"

"In the cuffs of his trousers there were traces of gravel that match that on the walkway of the bridge."

"Cuffs? Aren't they out of fashion?"

"They're back in. Not that it matters. Lennie was wearing khaki work pants from Sears and they have cuffs. The fact that gravel got in there suggests more than a casual stroll on the bridge."

"A struggle with Billy Herman? Wouldn't there have been some sign of that?"

"The pants had been washed, Roger. The gravel survived that. Lennie Miller took his clothes to a coin laundry. We know his habits. We know with fair certainty exactly where he washed those trousers."

"Then two things connect him with Billy Herman, the rifle and the gravel?"

"Three. The money. He still had the ten thousand Billy had paid him for the job."

"The same money?"

"The same." Keegan paused with a forkful of cannelloni before his face. "See what I mean, Roger? The thing just ties itself up. Norman Sheer's broker had the numbers of the bills recorded before handing them over to Norman. Why? He doesn't know. He just didn't like to see cash in large amounts being carried about by interns whose practical sense he distrusts. Perhaps there was a shakedown involved. Anyway, he records the serial numbers and they match those on the bills we found in Lennie Miller's pocket."

"How did you learn of the loan?"

"Norman. It wasn't easy for him either. He's more or less engaged to Sharon Herman. Not that we absolutely needed that information, what with the gun and gravel, but it makes it that much tighter. It's a good thing she sought Childers' advice.

" 'She' being Sharon Herman? What advice did he give her?"

"That she should tell us about the money. She had been stunned to learn from Norman that he had given her brother ten thousand dollars. The money had not been found after Billy's death. Where had it gone? She was hoping it provided a more acceptable explanation of his death. Robbery. I guess if you have a dead brother, you'd prefer to have him murdered than a suicide."

"The shot in the ball park?"

"Same gun."

"And Lennie wasn't working or somewhere else that day?"

Keegan shook his head. "He had the day off to go to the game. But he told Childers he was going to see the White Sox."

"They played out of town that day."

"I know. Obviously he wasn't a fan."

"Why would he mention a ball game at all?"

"The picture I get of Lennie Miller, he might have thought that was pretty cute. Ex-cons, Roger, have the damndest notion that they are way ahead of the rest of us. Don't ask me to explain it."

"Where do you get that picture of Lennie, from Mr. Childers?"

"Partly. Partly from his record. And from his parole officer, F. X. O'Boyle. You know him."

"Yes."

"Not that O'Boyle has given up on Lennie, even now. But he probably doubts that John Wilkes Booth shot Lincoln."

"I don't suppose you're relying on Mr. Childers alone to provide Lennie with an opportunity to be at the ball park that day."

Keegan frowned. "I'm more interested in the shot that didn't miss."

"Did anyone ever determine where the shot was taken from that day in the park?"

"It comes down to three possibilities."

"I suppose that was in the *Tribune*, but I didn't see it. What did all those people whose apartments overlook that park think, I wonder?"

Phil Keegan was impatient with this talk about Wrigley Field, and Roger Dowling did not really blame him. But the priest was having difficulty forming an image of Lennie Miller. Here was a young man, a significant fraction of whose life had been wasted in prison and whose job hardly required special skills—driving another man around—at the center of a most complicated set of events. A man who took his own washing to an automatic laundry. Roger Dowling had noticed such laundromats and been fascinated by them. There were always people in them, night or day, but more often than not the customers just sat listlessly while their clothes tumbled about in the machines. In the daytime, there would be mothers with young children, a family that could not afford its own washing machine.

But the natural clientele of such establishments were the single and the lonely. Were they also breeding places for assassins? Somehow Roger Dowling found that difficult to believe. But it was equally difficult to believe Billy Herman would hire a man to kill his father's enemy.

"Anybody is capable of anything, Roger," Phil Keegan said with obvious satisfaction.

"You may be right."

They adjourned to the study and a short session of cribbage, but Roger Dowling sensed he had dulled the triumph Phil Keegan felt at having a well-rounded solution to the murder of Aaron Leib. Who was he to question the plausibility of the solution? It did have a Shakespearian finality—bodies all over the stage, victims and assassins gone to that bourne from which no traveler returns. Shouldn't he derive some satisfaction from the fact that at least no poor devil faced the prospect of trial and imprisonment, with all the moral confusion involved? Of far more importance was the fact that Rosemary Walsh had come through this without her true identity becoming known.

Nonetheless, after Phil left, Roger Dowling sat at his desk and recalled the evening he and Phil had amused themselves by dreaming up a whole series of explanations of Leib's murder. Roger Dowling found it very difficult to believe Lennie Miller had been delivered over to the police with such conclusive evidence of guilt as the result of mere chance. Falling asleep in a garage with his motor running? Roger could not believe Keegan accepted that. Chance or suicide were the only explanations of Lennie's death that permitted Phil to close his file on the murder of Aaron Leib, and neither explanation seemed plausible. A contrite Lennie Miller, unable to live with the dreadful things he had done? But, suicide or accident, why in that garage? There was no garage where Lennie lived; there he parked in the street, so the garage in the basement of Childers' building was all he had. Roger Dowling didn't like it. But if it had not been chance or suicide, there was still an X to be identified.

Before going up to bed, he dialed Phil's number.

"Phil, when Lennie Miller was found, did you go over his car."

"You just don't like happy endings, do you, Roger?"

"Are there ever happy endings in matters like this?"

"It's being done now, Roger."

"And someone will calculate the volume of the garage, the density of the carbon monoxide, and the rest of it?"

"Yes, Roger. What are you getting at?"

"Are you really closing your file?"

"I want to, Roger. I really want to. There's only one hitch."

"What's that?"

"Robertson thinks I should."

F. X. O'Boyle, when Roger Dowling got him on the phone, said he had to be in court in the morning, but he could come to the rectory later, maybe around eleven.

"When do you usually have lunch?"

"Is that an invitation?"

"It is. I say Mass at noon. If you could come to the rectory about half past twelve...."

"I'll come to your Mass first."

"Good. Forgive me for calling you so late."

"You saved me the trouble of packing a lunch. I usually eat at my desk. Can you tell me what it's about, Father?"

"I want to know more about Lennie Miller."

O'Boyle's groan was painful to hear. "That poor guy. I was so sure..." But O'Boyle checked himself. "I'll see you in church, Father."

But it was only after the liturgy of the word, when Father Dowling was at the altar pouring wine into the chalice, that O'Boyle arrived at St. Hilary's. It would have been difficult to ignore his entrance. He burst through the doors and stood for a moment in the center aisle, looking around as if accustoming himself to the lesser light of the church. With his beard and generally disheveled look he might have alarmed the other worshipers, but those who attended the noon Mass were unlikely to be distracted. They had come to pray. A lesson there for me, Roger Dowling told himself. Phil Keegan, in his usual pew, was the only one who seemed aware of O'Boyle's entry.

Later, when he came out of the sacristy, Roger Dowling was not really surprised to find Phil and O'Boyle chatting on the walk that led to the rectory.

"Can you join us for lunch, Phil?"

"Oh," Phil said, but his surprise was not convincing. "O'Boyle's having lunch with you?"

"With us. Come on."

"You're sure I'm not butting in?"

Mrs. Murkin was always delighted when Roger Dowling had guests at his table, and not even the mild surprise that there would be two rather than one fazed her. Of course she probably regarded Phil Keegan as part of the household. Both guests exhibited the ravenous hunger Mrs. Murkin took to be the only adequate response to her labors in the kitchen.

"Now, there's plenty of everything, so don't be bashful."

Not even O'Boyle's wildly luxuriant beard bothered Marie, though Roger Dowling knew her feelings about unshaven men. Keegan told them about the preliminary results of the inspection of Lennie's car. It was possible, even in a garage of that size, for him to have died from carbon-monoxide poisoning whether by chance or design. Death had been effected by simply leaving the motor of the car running.

"But why the garage?"

O'Boyle said, "That's no surprise. I

expected him to head for home sooner or later."

"But he didn't live there, did he?"

"Home in a wide sense. He worked there. It was the center of his life. Not that I believe it was suicide."

"You don't?" Keegan said, but his tone did not invite O'Boyle to go on.

"No. I don't. I'll tell you something Lennie said to me. He had heard in Joliet from someone who worked with Anne and Archie that they had lost a lot of people. Where could they go? Most of them are wanted and are known to the police. How do you go underground from the underground, that's the problem. Change your name? Your face is known. You have a file on Anne and Archie, don't you, Captain? I'll bet it's full of people who have never been caught."

Keegan agreed, shooting a glance at Roger Dowling.

"So they must change their faces too. Now, remember, Anne and Archie claimed those killings."

Keegan grunted. "If Lennie told you that, it explains the phone calls. That's where he got the idea, thinking it would throw us off."

"But what if they're back in operation, Captain Keegan? With new names and new faces?"

"And what if the ones Lennie met in Joliet recruited him and he was simply doing their work?"

"You didn't know Lennie Miller. I did." O'Boyle looked stricken, the look of one who has lost a friend.

Roger Dowling decided to shut off this line of speculation. It would be worse than ironic if attention should be directed to Rosemary Walsh and cause her trouble now.

"The building where Lennie's body was found, he worked there?"

"For Lionel Childers." There were crumbs in O'Boyle's beard now. "He drove for him. Wonderful man."

"Isn't that unusual, hiring an ex-convict for a chauffeur?"

"You bet it is. Not many businessmen of the caliber of Lionel Childers would even consider it. He is the only one who actually did it."

"How did that come about?"

"I brought them together," O'Boyle said.

"Had Childers already indicated his willingness to employ an ex-convict?"

O'Boyle frowned. There was very little to see of his face except eyes and nose, yet he managed to convey a wide range of expressions. "I must have approached him about it. My memory isn't that clear."

"Could he have come to you?"

O'Boyle shook his head. "He wouldn't have known me."

"So you went to him. Why?"

O'Boyle said it was a campaign of his, pestering possible employers of his wards. It was a large part of his job, as he understood it, anyway. Had he visited Lionel Childers in his office? He thought for a moment, then shook his head. He didn't recall. Had Childers been in his office?

"Oh, yes."

"It sounds to me as if he must have made the first approach," Father Dowling said. "Now, isn't that curious?"

"If he did," Keegan said, impatient with this effort to be precise about the inconsequential, "O'Boyle doesn't seem to remember."

"However it came about, it's curious. Why should he hire an ex-convict?"

"Father, that's the prejudice I'm fighting."

"Fine, fine, but the prejudice is there.

Why was Lionel Childers so remarkably free of it?"

"Because he is an extraordinary man." O'Boyle looked back and forth from Keegan to Dowling. "Listen, I'll tell you something. In one way, from Captain Keegan's point of view, it might tell against Childers, but for the money it shows the kind of guy he is. After Leib was shot, Lennie disappeared. Then young Herman killed himself. Childers thought that, given Lennie's friendship with Billy Herman, he ought to report Lennie's absence. He came to me. The guy was really torn. He knew what would happen to Lennie if he got into trouble, and I don't mean murder, but just dropping out of sight that way. Childers asked me what he should do. He didn't want to cause trouble for Lennie. I told him to keep quiet."

"You're proud of that?" Keegan demanded.

"Yes, I am. For the simple reason that I knew Lennie could not have killed Aaron Leib. So I knew he couldn't have killed Billy Herman either."

"You *knew*, did you?"

O'Boyle nodded his head so violently the crumbs rearranged themselves in his beard.

325

"I knew. When Aaron Leib was shot, Lennie was having dinner with me at my home."

Phil Keegan fell back in his chair and Father Dowling too stared at the parole officer. O'Boyle took understandable pleasure from their reactions.

"Then why the hell didn't you let us know?"

"Let you know what? That a man you didn't even suspect was innocent? It's only since you found Lennie dead that you're so sure he killed two men. But I know he couldn't have killed the first man, so why would he have killed the second? That's why I told Lionel Childers he didn't have to report Lennie's absence. My only regret is that I didn't then and there go in search of Lennie."

"Why didn't you?"

"Childers asked me not to. He didn't want Lennie to think he was blowing the whistle on him. Even so, I could have kept Childers out of it. Maybe if I had found him he would be alive today."

Keegan had his notebook out and pointed a ballpoint pen at O'Boyle. "Okay. June eighteenth, Monday. Aaron Leib is shot on the golf course at approximately seven-thirty. Where were you at seven-thirty?"

"I would still have been at my office, I suppose. I don't often leave until..."

Keegan banged his pen down on his notebook. "You said you were having dinner with Lennie Miller at the time Aaron Leib was shot."

"But Lennie came by my office. From there we went to my home."

"What time did he come to your office?"

"When did you say Leib was shot?"

Keegan put his notebook and pen away. "Loyal O'Boyle. No wonder they call you that. If Lennie Miller were still alive, I bet you'd commit perjury for him."

"You did have dinner with Lennie that night?" Roger Dowling asked O'Boyle.

"Yes, I did, Father. And he did come to my office first and nobody can tell me he was fresh from the slaughter of Aaron Leib. I don't care about exact times and all that. Does anyone ever really know exact times? But there is no way Lennie Miller could have killed Leib and been at my office when he was and as he was. I mean his mood, his outlook."

"Maybe it was the seventeenth," Keegan

suggested sweetly.

O'Boyle spluttered, but there was in his indignation the uncertainty that Phil could be right. The parole officer had a very sympathetic memory, and that was too bad. If Lennie Miller had demonstrably come to see him and gone on with him to his home on the very day Aaron Leib was killed, that was very important, regardless of exact times. It was particularly important if Lennie was indeed the killer of Aaron Leib.

"How long did he stay?" Roger Dowling asked.

"We sat up drinking half the night."

Phil pushed back his chair and said he had to go. O'Boyle was in no hurry to leave and so, having shown Phil out (at the door, Keegan twirled a finger around one ear and rolled his eyes), Father Dowling stopped in the kitchen to fetch another bottle of beer for O'Boyle.

"Tell me, Francis, did Lennie ever speak to you of Billy Herman?"

O'Boyle sucked foam from his mustache. "Herman? No, we never talked about him."

"How often would you see Lennie?"

"He dropped around more than he had to. Maybe once a week."

"That often? And he never talked to you about Billy Herman? Did he talk about Lionel Childers?"

"Oh sure. And about his girl friend. Lennie was quite a talker."

"What did he think of Childers?"

O'Boyle paused. "Father, you have to understand about guys like Lennie. They need to knock everything and everybody. It's a way of establishing self-esteem. I know they think I'm some kind of clown, doing the work I do, making as little money as I do, even if it is helpful to them. Lennie used to kid around about Childers. It didn't mean a thing."

"Kid around how?"

Was O'Boyle blushing? He seemed to be. "About girls. Apparently Childers had some girl in an apartment in Chicago. Lennie got to know her and she told him stories about Childers. They sounded like a pair. Lennie and that girl."

"Who is she, I wonder?"

"What difference does it make?"

"Could you find out her name?"

"You really want to know who the girl was? I know her name. She's where I would have gone in search of Lennie.

If I had gone...."

"What is her name?"

"Rita."

"Rita what?"

"I don't know. He only used the first name."

"Then how could you have found her?"

"I would have found her, don't worry about that. Just from the sort of thing Lennie told me, I could have found her."

"Find her now, Francis. I want to talk to that girl."

O'Boyle was blushing again. Good heavens. "Francis, I'm inclined to agree with you about Lennie Miller. I certainly don't think he killed himself, whether deliberately or accidentally. Why would he? And if he didn't, the one who killed him is walking around free. But that isn't what really bothers me." Roger Dowling stopped, lest he become unctuous. "How corrupting of its doer the perfect crime is. And there are many perfect crimes. Perfect means only undetected by men. I do not regard that as much of an accomplishment."

"Father, if you really want to know, Lionel Childers..."

"No. No, I prefer not to bother him. I

gather he didn't know Lennie was having these chats with his paramour."

"I doubt that very much. I see what you mean. Okay, I'll find her."

Father Dowling hoped he would, but unfortunately Francis X. O'Boyle, scruffy, hirsute, sipping beer, did not inspire confidence. His claim to be able to provide an alibi for Lennie had crumbled so quickly after having been made so confidently that his assurance he could find the girl Rita seemed shakily based.

30

The chair behind his desk had served admirably as a vehicle in which to convey the inert Lennie Miller to the elevator and thus to the basement garage and his car. It was only when he had dumped Lennie rather unceremoniously in the back seat of the car and started its engine that Lionel Childers knew his first doubt concerning what he intended to do.

To drive out of this garage and through the city streets in Lennie Miller's car, and with Lennie unconscious behind him, suddenly seemed far more of a risk then he was prepared to take. There were far too many incalculable factors. That things had gone so well so far seemed reason for caution rather than for continued boldness. Indeed, sitting in Lennie's car, considering the things that might have gone wrong in the fairly simple operation of getting Lennie from his office to the garage, Lionel Childers felt a first tremor of fear. This was so uncustomary an emotion that he half enjoyed it, but his fear was retrospective, of what might have happened but had not. Prospective fear was a feeling he did not care for at all.

His desk chair stood there beside the car as if crying out to be noticed. If he were going to drive Lennie elsewhere, he must first get rid of that damned chair. No. Think. And, as it always had, thinking had its rewards. Lennie would be found here, in his own car, behind the wheel. The gas gauge registered three quarters full.

Childers got out of the car, took hold of Lennie's shoulders, and pulled him from the back seat. How heavy the little fellow was. Propped up behind the wheel, his head lolled and Childers eased it back. There was no need for Lennie to be uncomfortable. He was going on a very long journey indeed. Before shutting the door, Childers checked the cuffs of Lennie's trousers. The gravel, enough of it, was in place. Satisfied,

Childers wheeled his chair to the elevator and rode upward with a growing sense of relief.

Until he began to consider the things that might go wrong. Someone could enter the garage, notice the car with the running motor, investigate, discover Lennie, and sound the alarm. The thought of Lennie Miller awaking once more in the land of the living and the threat he posed was too much. Lionel Childers descended once more to the basement garage. In his hand he had a lengthy vacuum attachment filched from the maintenance room. He had a roll of masking tape too, should that be needed.

The basement was empty. The attachment fit neatly over the exhaust pipe. Childers introduced the other end of the hose into the wing window of the car and pushed it as far closed as he could. How long would it take? He had no idea. He sat in the basement, in his own car, for four hours before he detached the hose. There was no pulse in Lennie's wrist or throat. Fingerprints? Of course there would be fingerprints. But he did not think he would be called upon to explain them. He looked at Lennie one last time, almost solicitously. The circle was closed.

Confidence came and went in the course of the night and it was a struggle to prevent himself from going down to the basement again. Sometimes he thought himself fully capable of playing the role of the discoverer of the body and he imagined himself calling the police. But in his normally prudent moments, he knew that was beyond him. It was important to know where the line was, and not to cross it.

He was proud of the words he spoke when Lieutenant Horvath came to him with the news, words spontaneous and unrehearsed.

"Then he came back?"

Perfect.

And Horvath wanted to know what he meant and Childers permitted himself to be coaxed into saying he had not seen Lennie since the eighteenth. He could imagine O'Boyle corroborating this, and Howard Herman too, if Howard had registered Childer's complaint, uttered half a dozen times, that his driver seemed to have taken an unscheduled vacation.

"He had ten thousand dollars in his pocket," Horvath said.

"Good grief."

"Are you missing any money, Mr. Childers?"

"Ten thousand dollars? You flatter me, Lieutenant. I am not the sort of man who could keep that amount of cash lying about."

He did not respond to Horvath's inquiries as to where Lennie Miller might have laid hands on such a sum. He left that to Norman or Sharon. Norman came through, as why shouldn't he? He wanted his money back.

Afterward, he was able to refer to the friendship that had sprung up between Billy Herman and his chauffeur. The fact that he was the only one who seemed to know of their friendship no longer presented a risk. The numbers of the bills had been recorded: there was no doubt the money Lennie had in his pocket had come from Billy Herman.

The gravel was something he had debated with himself about. It seemed almost excessive, but, in the event, it was not. He found it in the cuffs of the trousers he had worn that day, a reminder of the fateful struggle on the bridge. Kept in an ash tray on his dressing table, he had never imagined he would find so inspired a use for it.

Questions were asked as to the nature of the falling out between Lennie and young Herman and, since the rules of the game were few and any number could play, theories proliferated, any one of which would have satisfied Lionel Childers. But their very abundance put the guilt of Lennie Miller beyond the reach of doubt.

And there was absolutely nothing that could possibly implicate Lionel Childers.

Post crimen triste? He did experience a lovely aching melancholy when he considered how absurdly well it had all turned out. Wilfrid Volkser's little band was completely routed in Congress, so there would be munitions contracts galore, and, with Aaron Leib gone, there was no doubt that Fox River Casing would get its share. Howard Herman, still in semi-shock over the death of Billy, had authorized Childers to proceed with the preparations for a stock issue. Without an heir, his interest in the fate of the business his father had founded was considerably diminished. Lionel foresaw little difficulty in easing Howard into an early retirement from the corporation Fox River Casing would soon become. Perhaps Howard would choose to devote his remaining energies to the cause of Israel?

The suggestion, dangerously close to being seen for the irony it was, struck a responsive chord. Howard saw in it redemption, of his own name, of his son's too, perhaps. And doubtless there was an opportunity, not consciously recognized, of a posthumous triumph over Aaron Leib.

Perfection, however, is boring. Great art is never perfectly symmetrical. Lionel Childers had need of a flaw and there was none. He half regretted not having provided one. Lennie might have, if he had explained to Rita the source of all that cash, but both had denied this and Lionel almost reluctantly believed them. Lennie would not have given such explosive information to Rita, and Rita, obsequious, pitifully eager to please, could not have withheld that gem from her campaign to ingratiate herself to Lionel Childers.

He would finance the cruise she was looking into and hope that with her undeniable talents she would be diverted from her present aspiration by a shipboard romance. If not, if she persisted, he would handle the problem decisively when the need arose.

Meanwhile, in the weeks remaining before she flew off to Miami to begin the cruise, Lionel would avail himself cautiously of Rita's charms, insisting they meet in the apartment as before.

"This place gives me the creeps, it really does. You don't know what it was like to come out of that bathroom and find him lying there with his hands behind his head, just looking at me. I was sure he meant to kill me."

"There, there," Lionel said absently. Babble was one of Rita's attractions, he didn't know why.

"Come with me on the cruise, Lionel. Please." Her nails on his bare chest were not the stimulant she seemed to imagine them, but he suffered her blandishments.

"I wish I could."

"You can. Why can't you?"

"Rita, you haven't the least notion how busy a man I am."

"I know you're important enough to be able to take a vacation when you want to."

"If only it were that simple."

"You could fly and meet the ship somewhere."

How odd to listen to these plans she made

for him. He had absolutely no intention or desire to go on a cruise with her. Rita, it was clear, could become a real pest, if he permitted it. But he did not mean to permit it.

So he lay there, smiling as she talked, turning over in his mind ways of easing Rita definitively from his life with a minimum of fuss and no hard feelings. It was almost as if Rita were the wanting flaw in the perfection he had achieved.

31

Francis X. O'Boyle did not expect Lionel Childers to mourn Lennie, exactly, but he thought maybe a little more sense of loss was in order. As for himself, he mourned Lennie in the only ways he knew: complaining about the system and having a Mass said for the repose of his soul. Yes, a Mass. It didn't matter that Lennie hadn't been a Catholic and that O'Boyle wasn't all that sure how much of it he himself still believed. Maybe it was just Celtic melancholy and a sense of fellowship with the dead, the great silent majority who have gone ahead of us into the dark.

Father Dowling did not want to accept a stipend for saying the memorial Mass but O'Boyle insisted. "My treat," Lennie had said, when he paid for the drinks. And that is what O'Boyle almost said to Roger Dowling. He didn't, of course, but if he had he was sure Father Dowling would have understood.

"Not that he believed in anything, Father."

"Oh, I doubt that. Chesterton said that when a man stops believing in God, he doesn't believe in nothing. He believes in anything."

"I don't think Lennie ever started."

"Well, we can't be sure of that. We can be sure that God believed in him."

That was a nice thought. Back in his office, O'Boyle had repeated it to himself and his throat constricted and his eyes filled with tears. He lit a cigar and wiped away his tears. Imagine what Lennie would have thought of his parole officer having prayers said for his soul and actually shedding tears for him. O'Boyle missed Lennie, he really did. It had always been fun when Lennie dropped by, to shoot the bull, have a drink, bum a free meal. A real wise apple, full of sly hints that Childers wasn't all that much of a big shot. Lennie had known more impressive people in Joliet. Sure he had.

Maybe that was the balance when you stopped to think of it. Lennie had never really grasped what a favor Childers had done him by hiring him as his driver, so why should Childers pretend that he was broken-hearted about Lennie's death?

"Don't get me wrong, O'Boyle, but I think it was very inconsiderate of him to pull that stunt in the basement of this building."

"He didn't have a garage," O'Boyle said.

Childers just stared at him shaking his head. "I suppose you have another ward who needs a job?"

"That really isn't why I came."

Childers moved things around on his desk as if he were playing some variant of chess. The huge uncluttered surface struck O'Boyle as a prop rather than a place where work was done. He associated work with mounds of paper, all the stuff you didn't want to file away because then you might forget it.

"What can I do for you, O'Boyle?"

The inspiration O'Boyle had counted on was not coming. He had as much as promised Father Dowling that he would not ask Childers for the name of the girl who had stolen money from Lennie. That was a promise easy to keep. He did not relish the thought of telling Lionel Childers that he knew he had a mistress in Chicago, one Lennie Miller had shared. He had come to Childers' office confident that something would occur to him that would lead Childers unwittingly to tell him the girl's name. Her last name. He remembered her first name was Rita.

"Would you be interested in hiring another parolee?"

"After my experience with Lennie, I'm not sure."

So they talked about that, the wisdom of hiring ex-cons, and still no inspiration came. When Childers asked him to send down his client for an interview it was clear that he had given O'Boyle as much time as he meant to.

"You understand I'm making no promises."

"I understand."

But what he understood was that he felt he had done Childers a favor by sending him Lennie rather than received one. Childers was like everybody else, finally; he did not really trust a man who had been to prison.

He found Rita through a contact on the Chicago vice squad. She worked out of a bar in Old Town and he did not find her until the second night. Sitting at the bar, nursing a Scotch and water while a girl the color of coffee danced nude on the diminutive stage, O'Boyle growled at the girls who came up to him asking if he wanted company. This is what they did when they were not up there dancing themselves. Behind him, in the dimly-lit booths, varieties of sexual business were being transacted. O'Boyle had felt some excitement the first night, marveling at the lovely bodies of the girls as they contorted in the smoky spotlight. But the second night he felt revulsion and then a vast sadness. How joyless the life of pleasure was. Hard, pushy hookers and skulking shamefaced men. And the noise. Why was it easy to believe in God in places where he seemed most absent?"

He recognized Rita from the photograph he had been shown and, when she looked down the bar at him, he was almost sure she would recognize him as a friend of Lennie. Her eyes cut through him, drifted on, returned. O'Boyle turned away. He was embarrassed, as if he were letting down Lennie by tracking down his girl. O'Boyle was sure the girl missed Lennie from the stories Lennie had told him. The money?

Lennie had not really blamed Rita; he had been an idiot giving her a chance at his cash. A couple of hundred bucks. Lennie had dismissed it with a shrug and a lopsided grin and there was affection in his voice when he spoke of Rita.

When he turned to look at her again she was talking with a man. He was middle-aged, bald, sheepish, and the topic of their conversation was unmistakable. The man bought her a drink and pulled his stool closer. O'Boyle involuntarily was shocked. Of course this was Rita's job, but it seemed disloyal to Lennie to carry on like this so soon after his death. The night before, O'Boyle had imagined Rita sitting abject in her apartment, wherever it was, disconsolate, probably drunk, crying for Lennie Miller. She was laughing now, a throaty sexy laugh and the bald-headed man smiled shyly. O'Boyle was struck by Rita's icy eyes, no matter the laughter and constant smile.

O'Boyle left, got his car out of the bar's pay lot and was waiting when Rita and her client emerged from the bar. She hailed a cab with a practiced wave and O'Boyle followed. But they went to a hotel of the kind that caters to girls like Rita. That would not be where she lived. He drove back to the bar and half an hour later she returned. At three o'clock, after four more round trips, Rita emerged from the bar alone. She set off on foot and walked several blocks before she hailed a cab. It was incredible to O'Boyle that she was unaware of the way he had haunted her evening.

After she disappeared into the building where the cab left her, O'Boyle waited for a light to go on upstairs. At that hour it was the only lighted window in the building. Then he checked the doorbells and her name leapt out at him. Lennie must have mentioned it. Rita Cassidy. O'Boyle went home to his silent house and the sound of his sleeping children and the even breathing of his wife seemed a music of ineffable innocence. The next day he telephoned Father Dowling.

32

"I've traced the girl," O'Boyle said on the phone. "She has an apartment on the near north side."

"Have you spoken to her?"

"No."

"What is the address of the apartment?"

He wrote down the address and the girl's name. Rita Cassidy. The name suggested she was or had been Catholic and Father Dowling wondered if that was advantageous. The fallen-away Catholic often harbors, not always without reason, resentments of the wildest kind, usually against priests and nuns.

"I don't know if Childers is still seeing her."

"You didn't get this information from

him, did you?"

"You said not to." O'Boyle sounded hurt. "It wasn't easy."

"I'm sure it wasn't. And I'm grateful to you."

"Can I ask why you want to see her?"

"I'm not really sure. Perhaps she can tell me something that will justify your faith in Lennie Miller." Roger Dowling did not emphasize the perhaps, but he was inclined to agree with Phil Keegan that it was doubtful Lennie had been a victim.

"I'll come with you, Father."

"That isn't necessary."

"I want to. You understand the kind of girl she is?"

Roger Dowling said he understood. He realized that O'Boyle's offer to accompany him to Rita Cassidy's was protective. Their visit would best be made now, this afternoon.

"She works nights," O'Boyle added, his voice odd.

After he had hung up, Roger Dowling picked up his breviary and read with less than complete attention vespers for the day. When he closed the book on his finger he let his eyes drift across the study to the bookshelves. He no longer resisted the thoughts that had been relentlessly forming in his mind during the previous week. The problem was how to verify them. When the call came from O'Boyle's office, indicating that the parole officer would be delayed, it was unclear for how long, Father Dowling decided to pay the visit alone.

From a drugstore a block from her apartment, Roger Dowling telephoned Rita Cassidy and asked if he might come see her. It was a relief to hear her voice, not only to learn she was at home, but to find she was indeed real.

"Roger Dowling? Do I know you?"

"We have a mutual friend. Lionel Childers."

"Oh." The word was prolonged but it was difficult to know what her reaction was. "Did Lionel give you my number?"

"That's not likely, is it?"

She hung up. Roger Dowling was startled. Had anyone ever hung up on him before? Certainly not in years. What a genteel world he inhabited. He came out of the booth almost sheepishly. Walking up the street through what seemed an innocent enough neighborhood, he reflected that his destination was such that his visit could be misinterpreted. He thought vaguely of scandal, of prudence and caution and the rest. He thought of Cardinal Danielou, who had been found dead in the apartment of a woman not above suspicion. One's reaction to such news was a revelation of one's character. If it were known that Father Dowling meant to visit a kept woman on the near north side, how many would assume he was there in his capacity as a priest? How many would think he had overcome drinking only to succumb to another weakness? Perhaps he would not even succeed in paying his visit on Rita Cassidy.

At the building he hesitated before the array of bells. Cassidy was there, as big as life, but would she trip the lock in response to his voice? He splayed his hands and pressed eight buttons at once, feeling he was playing the accordion. A distant chorus of voices spoke.

"Father Roger Dowling," he said, some urgency in his voice.

The buzzer sounded and he pushed the door open. At least he had not entered on completely false pretenses. He took the elevator to the top floor, then started down the stairs, checking names beside doors, fearful that one of those who had accommodated his ring might be looking into the hall in expectation. And indeed that is just what happened on the first floor below the top.

A woman in middle age, tall, thin, her steel-gray hair done in tight painful-looking curls, was half emerged from her doorway.

"Was it you who rang below?"

"Yes. I seem to have pressed the wrong button. I'm looking for Rita Cassidy."

Did the woman's manner turn hostile? She pointed downward, thrusting a finger at the floor, the gesture both a direction and a seeming condemnation. Her door slammed behind her. Well, that was one reaction to his visit to Rita Cassidy.

The name Rita Cassidy was on a card inserted in a metal frame on her door. Father Dowling rapped briskly.

The door opened almost immediately and for a wild moment Roger Dowling thought he was going to be greeted with an embrace. Instinctively, he stepped back. The girl stopped herself and her eyes widened.

"I'm Roger Dowling."

"Good God, you're a priest!"

"That's right."

"But I...How did you happen to know ...Father, I'm not a Catholic any more. Not for years."

"I'm sorry to hear it. But that's not why I'm here. I told you on the phone I know Lionel Childers."

"Now, look here, Father."

"May I come in? Please? I never met Lennie Miller but I know a good deal about him."

"Lennie!"

In her confusion, she let him in. He walked past her into the living room and was seated and filling his pipe when she came in. "Do you mind?" he asked, flourishing his pipe.

"Oh, not at all. Make yourself right at home." But he could see that his collar made sarcasm difficult for her. "Who told you about me?"

He lit his pipe, deliberately, and she decided to sit down.

"You say you know Lionel?"

"I've met him, yes." His pipe was drawing well and he sat back. "Like Mr. Childers, I am from Fox River. Lennie Miller lived there too. You have heard that he is dead?"

"I heard."

"Could we talk a bit about him? I understand you knew him well, so perhaps only you know the answers to certain questions."

"I don't have to talk to you, you know. You more or less forced your way in here. I don't have to say a thing."

"No, you don't. But why on earth wouldn't you?"

"I don't know. What are the questions?"

"Since I have no way of knowing how much you've heard or read of recent events in Fox River, let me summarize them for you. On June sixteenth a shot was fired in Wrigley Field, apparently at the Israeli consul."

"Wrigley Field isn't in Fox River."

He smiled. "No. But the Fox River Country Club, as its name implies, is. On June eighteenth a man was shot and killed while golfing there. Aaron Leib. He had been in the box with the Israeli consul at Wrigley Field."

"You sound like a cop. Why are you asking me questions?"

"I really haven't asked you any yet.

Lennie Miller is thought to have killed Aaron Leib as well as another man, Billy Herman."

"I believe it."

"Now you sound like the police. Why do you say that?"

"Because I know the kind of man he was. He was vicious, cruel, mean."

"Did he ever speak to you about killing these men?"

"No!"

"When did you last see him?"

She looked at the ceiling and he could see lies form like cumulus clouds in her eyes.

"What time was it that you saw him on June eighteenth? Let's start with that."

"June eighteenth?"

"Yes. He had had dinner with a Mr. O'Boyle and they sat up late drinking..."

"I saw him that morning."

"The morning of the eighteenth?"

"No, the morning after he'd been drinking like that. He showed up here, don't ask me why, and I was afraid he'd wake up the whole building, so I let him in. The way he was I was afraid not to." She paused, but only for a minute. "As soon as he fell asleep, I left. I was so scared I spent several days in a hotel. I figured he would just go away for good."

"Several days?"

"Two nights, nearly three days."

"And when you came back?"

"He was gone."

From the way she spoke, Roger Dowling did not believe that, but he decided not to force the issue. She was far more forthcoming than he had hoped, particularly after she had hung up on him.

"How frightened you must have been to stay away from your own apartment for nearly three whole days."

"I was very frightened, Father. I told you he was a mean, cruel person."

"Had he ever struck you?"

"Yes." Immediately she regretted having said that, but he let it go.

"Didn't you have anyone to call, anyone you might have gone to?" The question, even more than he had intended, suggested a person so bereft of friends, so utterly alone, that her single recourse when frightened had been the anonymity of a hotel.

"Well, I had Lionel."

"What did he say when you called him?"

"Well, he...I didn't say I called him."

"But you did call him, didn't you?"

"Father, I don't want to be questioned like this. I don't know what you're after, but I think you're trying to trip me up and get me to say something. Something that isn't true. And I won't stand for that."

There was the sound of a key in the lock and Rita leaped to her feet.

"You're going to have to go now." She glanced wildly toward the sound of the turning key. The door was pushed open.

"Rita," a voice called. "It's me."

And then Lionel Childers stood in the door of the little living room. Rita ran to him as if to block his view of the priest, but the eyes of the two men had already met and Roger Dowling could not tell if he was recognized or not. He had remained seated.

"You're busy," Childers said, beginning to back out.

"No! I'm not. He's going. Aren't you, Father? He just stopped by."

"We met at the Hermans, Mr. Childers," Roger Dowling said, and Childers stopped backing away. He pulled his hand free from Rita's.

"Isn't this out of your territory, Father?"

"The Archdiocese of Chicago is a very

large place, Mr. Childers. I have been asking Rita some questions about your late chauffeur, Lennie Miller."

"Have you?" Childers unbuttoned his jacket and looked around. He seemed undecided whether to seem a stranger here or to show that he knew the place well. He sat down and ignored Rita when she asked if he would like a drink. "Poor Lennie, I had hoped he had mended his ways. I'm afraid I'm not much of a judge of character, Father Dowling."

"You remember my name? I'm pleased. I find it very difficult to believe you're a poor judge of character. I should think that would be a great handicap in business."

"You're right. But Lennie was a new type to me. He had been in prison, you know."

"So I understand. But Francis X. O'Boyle thought very highly of him."

Childers' brows went up. "So you know O'Boyle too?"

"A priest becomes acquainted with a great many people."

"And where did you run into Rita?"

"Lionel, he just came. I've never seen him before. He telephoned first and then..."

He had not told her to shut up, but his

expression sufficed. He turned back to Father Dowling. "Assuming you don't go around randomly ringing doorbells, what brought you here?"

"Well, I am having difficulty accepting the seemingly official version of the Aaron Leib and Billy Herman killings. According to that version, Lennie Miller killed them both."

"Yes, I know." Childers settled back. "It is even harder for me to believe, Father, I assure you. I knew Lennie..."

"And now Lennie himself is dead."

Childers shook his head sadly. "Well, after all, having killed two men, his remorse must have been a heavy thing. Not that I presume to instruct the clergy on the nature of remorse. You're more or less of a professional in the sense of guilt, aren't you, Father?"

"More or less. Speaking professionally, I would find it more plausible if Lennie had decided to spend some of that money found on him rather than kill himself."

"Did Judas spend the thirty pieces of silver?" Childers asked. He sounded like a deacon. Or the devil.

Father Dowling chose not to notice the

distasteful parallel. On the point of saying Judas had killed himself, he stopped. That was not the way to get through Childers' sophisticated defense system. Father Dowling found his curiosity about Lionel Childers increasing. The fact that Childers had shown up at Rita's apartment was already a link with Lennie Miller.

"What has struck me in all this," Father Dowling said musingly, "is that the attention of the police has not been turned on you."

"Father Dowling, I assure you I have spent many hours with the police since Lennie's body was found."

"No doubt. But that is not the kind of attention I meant." Roger Dowling considered the bowl of his pipe; the fire had gone out. He tamped down the ashes. "You must wonder what brings me here to Miss Cassidy's apartment."

"I believe I've already expressed my surprise."

"I have a habit, a bad habit, I admit it, of becoming occupied with police investigations. My excuse is that, having friends who are policemen, I hear more than one perhaps should of the matters they are inquiring into. But that is all it is, an excuse. I just can't stop myself from speculating about the police's quarry. To them he is a criminal who must be brought to justice. Yet he remains a human being and—forgive me for speaking professionally, Mr. Childers—a human being is the object of an infinite forgiving love."

Childers' frown was the deferential expression of the layman when embarrassing topics are introduced. "If I may say so, Father, my own attitude toward Lennie was not unlike your own. A man who has been in prison...well, not many care to trust him."

"Yes, I see what you mean. Your tolerance was all the more generous given Miss Cassidy's rather grim description of Lennie's personality."

"How far had you gotten in your discussion of Lennie?" Childers shot a cold glance at Rita.

"And then to have his body found in the basement of the building in which you live and work," Father Dowling said. "That is when I began to worry about you, Mr. Childers."

"Worry about me?" Childers' chuckle was a product of surprise and delight.

"Yes. Just think of it. It was as if someone were deliberately pointing to the central role you have played in these events."

"I'm not sure I know what you mean, Father."

"It's perfectly obvious. What is the official version of what happened? Billy Herman paid Lennie Miller ten thousand dollars to shoot Aaron Leib. It would occur to one to wonder how young Herman came to know Lennie Miller."

"They were close, Father. Thick as thieves. I have testified to that."

"Indeed you have. Using just that phrase, I understand. 'Thick as thieves.' It casts a sort of light on that fictitious friendship, doesn't it?"

"Fictitious?"

"I am explaining my fears on your behalf. Who else said anything or, if asked, knew anything about a friendship between these two men? No one. You are the only one who knew of it. Its existence depends solely on your say-so."

"I assure you it's true, Father."

"It had better be true, hadn't it? It is such an essential part of the official version of events. What will become of you when it occurs to someone that this essential part cannot be verified, apart from your testimony? O'Boyle had never heard of it, yet he knew Lennie Miller well. Sharon Herman had never heard of it, though she and her brother were close. And no one seems ever to have seen the two men together."

"I'm sure they were very careful, once they had struck their bargain."

"Except with you. I wonder why. It's as if...No. Then you went to O'Boyle to report on Lennie's absence after the shooting of Aaron Leib."

"That was said in confidence. I did not want to bring harm to Lennie."

"You had no idea where he might have gone? Didn't Miss Cassidy phone and tell you he had come here?"

"Here!" Childers glared at Rita and she turned to Roger Dowling as to the lesser of two evils.

"Did Lennie have the money with him when he came here, Rita?"

"How would I know?"

"Lennie did not come here," Lionel Childers said emphatically. "You are correct in assuming Rita would have informed me if Lennie had come here. She did not."

"Why didn't you tell Mr. Childers, Rita?"

"I don't have to answer your damned questions," she cried.

"She's right, you know," Childers said. He attempted a laugh. "Don't get me wrong. I admire your attitude, Father Dowling. I only wish Lennie had been more deserving of such trust. From both of us."

Dowling ignored this. "You said Lennie arrived here drunk, Rita. That was early in the morning of the nineteenth, perhaps not twelve hours after he had shot and killed a man. Did he appear to you to be a murderer?"

"He was drunk. He seemed drunk."

"But later, after you learned what Lennie had done, what did you think of his visit then? Did he have a rifle with him when he came here?"

"No!"

"A pistol, then?"

"He didn't have any gun at all."

Dowling nodded. "And no money either?"

"I don't know."

"Very well. Let's suppose then that he didn't have the ten thousand dollars he was paid to kill Aaron Leib. Really, I don't see how he could have had it."

Childers, arms folded, legs crossed, looked sternly at Roger Dowling. "Why not?"

"Would Billy Herman have given him the money before he shot Aaron Leib? That seems unlikely, given the prejudice that exists against men with Lennie's background. Your point, Mr. Childers. So when would he have received the money?"

Childers smiled. "I don't see the problem. He came here to Rita's apartment early the following morning. The shooting took place in the early evening, didn't it? That allows plenty of time..."

"But all the intervening time is accounted for. He spent it with Francis O'Boyle."

"He did?"

"Yes. So you see that he could not possibly have had the money with him when he came here to Rita's."

Roger Dowling sat back, as if in triumph, and Rita and Childers exchanged a glance that could not completely conceal amusement.

"That does seem logical, Father Dowling."

"I know. And what if it were true as well?"

"Why can't it be?"

"Because then there was no chance at all

for Lennie to get the money from Billy Herman. A few days later Billy himself was dead."

"That's right. A few days. More than ample time in which to arrange the payoff. Perhaps turning over the money and getting killed happened at the same time."

"That's what I thought might have happened. But it could not have."

"Unless I am mistaken, the police are convinced it did."

"But they also know that Lennie Miller was in a room in the Chicago YMCA at the very time Billy Herman was killed."

"Does anyone know that? It's the first I've heard of it."

"O'Boyle went to see him. They were together when Billy Herman was killed."

"O'Boyle hasn't told this to the police."

"I'm not sure he realizes it himself." Roger Dowling had to rely on O'Boyle's admittedly wavering memory for the exact day he had visited Lennie at the Y.

"But you do?"

"You can appreciate why I began to grow concerned for you, Mr. Childers."

"There is no problem if, contrary to your inference, Lennie had the money with him when he came here to Rita's."

"But you agreed that is illogical."

"He had it," Rita said. "He had ten thousand dollars in an envelope. I saw it."

"Shut up," Childers snapped. He tried unsuccessfully to smile at Father Dowling. "Your hobby in contagious. Obviously Rita is a very susceptible player."

Father Dowling closed his eyes and began to nod vigorously. "Yes. She took the money. That's it." He opened his eyes and looked at Rita. "You took the money with you when you left to spend those three days in a hotel. When did you return it to Mr. Childers?"

"That's enough, Father Dowling. I have ceased to find this amusing."

"I should think so. Did Lennie come to you for the money Rita had taken from him? Is that the explanation of his being found in the basement of your building? Dead?"

Childers stood. "A bit of advice, Father Dowling. It would be defamation of character for you to engage in this parlor game with people who might mistakenly take you seriously. Needless to say, I don't like the implications of what you're saying. It is one thing to indulge you here. I assure you I will show no such tolerance if you should talk like this elsewhere."

Father Dowling met his gaze. "Think of all those whose trust you have betrayed. Lennie Miller. Billy Herman. His father. How many others? And you are not yet done, are you? You will continue to betray Howard Herman's trust. And I suppose Rita too is expendable."

"I have warned you, Father Dowling."

"Oh, it's far too late for that. As soon as you walked into this apartment it was too late. That was one entrance too many, Mr. Childers. If you had stayed away, you might conceivably have kept suspicion from yourself. But it is one coincidence too many."

"Are you threatening to spread these crazy theories?"

"And thus effect your arrest and conviction? That will be done whatever I may do. You should not underestimate the police, Mr. Childers."

The buzzer sounded and Childers wheeled as if the police were there on Dowling's cue. But when he decided to have Rita answer, it was the voice of O'Boyle that mingled with the street sounds below.

"Miss Cassidy? My name is O'Boyle. I was a friend of Lennie Miller."

"We're leaving," Childers said to Roger Dowling. "Come. I'll give you a lift in my car."

"I have my own."

"Come on!"

Roger Dowling got up. "Very well." Lionel Childers was truly shaken at last. His defenses had crumbled. He had become a man one might pity.

Childers guided Roger Dowling by the elbow to the staircase and they started down. They got as far as the second landing before they came face to face with Lieutenant Horvath, puffing up the stairs.

"You taking him in, Father Dowling?"

That Childers' elaborate and murderous plans should have led to a try at humor on the part of Cy Horvath was the beginning of the end. Beyond humor, Lionel Childers tried to force his way past Horvath. The struggle was brief. Watching a subdued Childers being led away in handcuffs, Roger Dowling felt genuine pity for the man. He remounted the stairs to the apartment where O'Boyle, Keegan, and a Chicago detective were assuring the hysterical Rita Cassidy everything was going to be all right. In the context, the remark had the ring of a primal lie.

33

"Howard Herman," Phil Keegan said, squinting through cigar smoke at Roger Dowling.

"What made him suspect Childers?"

"Of murder? He didn't. To get over his grief he decided to get back to work. Childers' designs on his company were what turned the trick. He hired a lawyer to look into Childers. It was something he should have done a long time ago. He got himself a sleazy lawyer to handle a sleazy assignment." Keegan drew on his cigar. "Tuttle."

"Would you like another beer?"

"I'm fine."

They sat in Roger Dowling's study in the St. Hilary rectory. From the kitchen came the sounds of Mrs. Murkin, cleaning up in preparation for going to bed.

"Tuttle suspected Childers?"

"Not of murder. No, it was something that occured to Herman after a talk with Tuttle. So Herman came to me."

Roger Dowling puffed on his pipe, waiting. The fact that Phil was stretching it out was good. Phil had every reason to be angry with him for going to Rita Cassidy's apartment and provoking Lionel Childers.

"The man had killed three people, Roger. Two with his own hands."

"I know."

"You know now."

Dowling had not pressed the point. His knowledge had been a hunch but nonetheless certain for that. As it turned out, it was the same thing that had directed Phil Keegan and Cy Horvath to Lionel Childers.

"Herman asked me why we had gone to see Childers before coming to him when we were looking for Billy. I told him we hadn't. He had suspected that Tuttle was Childers' source for what we were doing. The man hangs around headquarters as if he had an office there."

"And it dawned on you that only Childers claimed to know of a link between young

Herman and Lennie Miller."

"That's right."

Marie Murkin looked in on them. "I'm turning in, Father. Can I get either of you anything?"

"You saved his life, Marie. That's enough for one day."

Marie denied the accolade, though she was clearly pleased by what Phil had said. God only knew what would have happened if Marie had not told Phil that Roger Dowling had gone to see O'Boyle. The bearded parole officer led the police to Rita Cassidy's apartment.

"I'm just grateful that he's safe, Captain."

"Me too. I was worried he'd miss our date tomorrow."

Roger Dowling looked at Phil. "When did we . . ."

"Now. I thought we could shoot a round of golf."

"It'll have to be early."

In the doorway, Marie gasped. "For heaven's sake! Have you forgotten what happened to Aaron Leib?"

The two men laughed and Mrs. Murkin went off to her room. The hazards of golf: ordeal by water, treacherous sand, the fatal lure of the rough as one hooked and sliced his way to the indented destination. Phil told the story of the man whose main objection to being housebound was that he kept hitting the ceiling with his club. But this was no time to exchange golf stories. Not if they were going to tee off at nine o'clock.

Later, after Phil had gone, Roger Dowling lit a final pipe and thought of Marie's equating of golf and danger. Danger did lurk in unexpected places: Cub Park, the Stratton Bridge, the fifteenth hole of the Fox River Country Club. It was an odd thought that a golf course too lies in the Vale of Tears. Where else? It is the only real estate there is.

Before getting into bed, Father Dowling took a club from his bag and practised his grip. He brought the club back slowly, then stopped. He couldn't take a full swing. He didn't want to hit the ceiling.